"Freeze!" Carter cried. He wanted this one alive.

The panicked attacker stopped and stood frozen for a moment with his back to Carter. He seemed to shudder, his shoulders shaking as if crying. Then he turned.

The fear was like a twisted mask on his small, dark face. But pride was there too. Pride, and shame, and in the eyes a tortured fanaticism.

He raised the Uzi and cried out in Hindi, "Krishna is great!" The Killmaster had no choice, and fired twice.

Flung backward like a rag doll, the small man sprawled on his back on the street, the Uzi firing one last burst into the sky as his finger tightened convulsively on the trigger.

Then there was only silence.

NICK CARTER IS IT!

FROM THE NICK CARTER
KILLMASTER SERIES

ARMS OF VENGEANCE

KILL MASTER

NICK CARTER

JOVE BOOKS, NEW YORK

KILLMASTER #255: ARMS OF VENGEANCE

A Jove Book / published by arrangement with
The Condé Nast Publications, Inc.

PRINTING HISTORY
Jove edition / November 1989

ISBN: 0-515-10171-0

Jove Books are published by The Berkley Publishing Group,
200 Madison Avenue, New York, New York 10016.
The name "JOVE" and the "J" logo
are trademarks belonging to Jove Publications, Inc.

PRINTED IN THE UNITED STATES OF AMERICA

10 9 8 7 6 5 4 3 2 1

Dedicated to the men and women of the
Secret Services of the
United States of America

PROLOGUE

Los Angeles

The new display rooms were a great joy. Everything about the completely refurbished Los Angeles Museum of Art excited Ramdass Ghosh. There were ample tracks for lighting fixtures. There was abundant floor space. The shelving was generous. The natural lighting from the ceiling and walls invited a creative display that encompassed the very largest to the very smallest pieces.

And no doubt about it, this display would have some of the largest and smallest significant pieces in the world today. Ramdass Ghosh was thrilled as he reached into another crate and brought out a two-foot terra-cotta statue of a dancing Shiva, the lord of the universe.

Ghosh had put in time in schools in his native India, here in the States, and in Italy and France. Even though he had long been a U.S. citizen, and had become Americanized to such things as Marlboro Lights, Plymouths, and the L.A. Raiders, the appreciation of the arts and traditions of his

1

native country were still the source of his greatest pleasure.

A papier-mâché representation of the goddess Kali, almost comic-book-like in its simplicity and bright colors, gave him a simultaneous smile of amusement at the brashness and a deep stirring of respect at the power inherent in it. Any number of persons were fearful of Kali because of her associations with death and change, and because she was traditionally pictured wearing a macabre necklace of human skulls.

But Ghosh was not superstitious, and he knew that Kali also represented the creative force.

Not strictly a religious man now, Ghosh set the Kali down and again handled the statue of the lord of the universe. He touched it reverently, remembering how Shiva was the chosen god of his family. All his relatives were fond of Kali and Krishna and even his own namesake, Rama, but when it came down to it, Shiva took the place of special fondness.

The intimate feelings for Shiva were a family tradition.

This statue was a particularly fine specimen nearly a thousand years old, well cast, the limbs lithe and athletic. Ghosh decided to give it a particularly commanding spot in the display.

Following his notebook of preliminary sketches, he opened more crates and set out pieces. He did not notice for some time that the door to the gallery had opened, and a young woman in the distinctive maroon smock of the museum docent—the volunteer curator—watched him.

When at last he saw her, Ghosh felt his heartbeat quicken.

He'd been watching her for days, intrigued by her fine-featured beauty, her long dark hair pulled into a tight bun, her neat legs, and her elegant posture.

Perhaps she was liberated enough so that an arranged marriage was not something with which she had to cope.

Ghosh took a look at the fine swell of her breasts and found himself thinking about the future. His family had stopped pressuring him to accept an arranged marriage to an

Indian girl. They might now accept whatever young woman he chose.

He considered the beautiful museum docent, the only other person in the cavernous display room. He would like to choose her. Yes, most definitely. And as an American it might be better for him if she were not, as he suspected, Indian, but instead a dark-skinned product of the great U.S. melting pot.

His detail-oriented eyes sought and found her left hand. No wedding ring.

Another flip-flop for the heart of Ramdass Ghosh.

Her eyes met his and he was stunned by his desire for her. Some of his friends from Calcutta had confessed a longing for the blond-haired, blue-eyed type of woman. But Ghosh still preferred a darker, more exotic beauty. Especially one like this.

The large room was air-conditioned, but even so, Ghosh noticed the sudden eruption of a fine row of sweat on her upper lip. She, too, was excited. Could it be that she'd been attracted to him and had finally brought herself to approach him?

"You are perhaps liking the subject of this exhibition?" Ramdass Ghosh asked. "You would perhaps enjoy helping to set it up?"

A rueful smile played on her full lips. "I can't let you do this," she said. "I simply can't." She reached into a large, thin leather bag, withdrew a Ruger Mini 14, and popped off a shot. It caught Ghosh squarely between the eyes.

ONE

Dallas, Texas

When the waitress served Nick Carter his dinner, she leaned closer and let him see her cleavage. "Y'all want anythin' else?" she asked. "Anutha beer? Maybe somethin' more fancy?"

Carter shook his head, trying to be inconspicuous as he continued to observe Porter Perrine, who sat at a nearby booth chomping lamb curry, completely unaware that he was about to be murdered.

Part of Carter's inconspicuous look was the way he was dressed—as an affluent, good ol' boy Texan, with a pin-striped suit and bolo tie. His white brocade dress shirt was custom made at a small shop in the Adolphus Hotel. His lizard-skin boots went for fourteen hundred at the Nieman-Marcus in the Galleria.

Agent Nick Carter worked for AXE, a supersecret espionage organization so select that few beyond its head and founder, David Hawk, knew its exact structure and

5

functions. Carter knew that Hawk occasionally got his
instructions from the president of the United States. Hawk
had given Carter the designation Killmaster N3—licensed
to kill in the service of his country.

All week, Carter had been told to watch Porter Perrine,
the chubby Texas industrialist. Check Perrine's movements.
Note all contacts and activities. Take no other action. Carter
was not even supposed to contact David Hawk for two more
days.

And although it had not been said in so many words,
Carter knew that he was not to do anything more than look
at the leggy brunette sitting on the other side of the room
who was obviously bored with her boyfriend and interested
in Carter. Spoiled rich kid from SMU or the University of
Texas, probably an old-timer with the state ritual of a
drive-in movie and a case of Pearl beer since she was fifteen
and a little man-crazy. But off limits for Carter now.

Right here, in the main dining room of the Star of India,
one of the poshest restaurants in Dallas, a bearded man who
wore aviator-frame glasses and went by the name of Bruce
Campbell was preparing his weapon to take out Perrine.
Supremely confident, and certainly unaware of Carter's
surveillance because avoiding detection was one of the
things Carter did so well. It was rumored you couldn't even
talk to Campbell about an elimination for less than a
million.

Carter checked his watch. He'd be able to tell Hawk
everything—who Perrine had seen that day, where Perrine
had been sitting in the Star of India, who got him, what the
weapon was, what the time of death was. And of course the
name of the assassin.

Across the room the brunette raised her voice, then
gracefully tossed about five dollars' worth of Jack Daniel's
and some Perrier ice cubes into the face of her date. She
sprang huffily to her feet.

She threaded her way through the tables, tall and well
coordinated. She was heading in his direction. Not as young

as she'd appeared at a distance. Packing a certain sensual maturity.

Carter stiffened for action. It was all going to happen at once.

Campbell had his weapon—a small, deadly blowgun—ready. It looked much like an expensive cigarette holder. Campbell even had some fancy cigarettes, some Balkan Sobranies, on the table as a ruse. He leaned over and blew through the blowgun. Apparently satisfied, he fit a small dart in it.

The brunette approached Carter's table. There was something vaguely foreign about her. She had probably taken some acting lessons. Without lowering her head, she gazed down at him. He glanced up, impressed with her aggressiveness. Under different circumstances he would have been pleased, jumping to his feet to invite her to sit.

Her lips parted and her voice projected directly and clearly to him in a powerful whisper. But it was unlikely anyone else could hear her.

"You need to get out of here right now!" she told him. "You need to call a cigar-smoking friend. You need to get out of this building and call from the parking lot. Move!" She passed by Carter with a liquid sway of magnificent hips, heading directly toward the door.

Carter stood immediately. The brunette's message was filled with insider knowledge. The cigar-smoking friend was Hawk, who had undoubtedly deputized her to get Carter to make contact sooner than planned. In fact, immediately.

He watched Porter Perrine bat a hand toward his neck as if swatting a mosquito. The dart had been delivered silently, perfectly.

Carter continued toward the door, aware that Perrine would be dead in a matter of moments. There was nothing anyone could do about it.

Nearby, Campbell lazily fit a Balkan Sobranie cigarette into the blowgun.

Ahead of him the leggy brunette with the magnificent

hips increased her pace. She looked like a lady in a hurry to get somewhere or to get away from somewhere. Automatically Carter sped up too.

She rounded the corner by the maître d's stand and disappeared from Carter's sight. The officious-looking maître d' in his plumed turban offered some comment, but she gave no acknowledgment, just kept moving.

In the parking area, she was nowhere in sight. Vanished as if she'd had a car waiting. Very suspicious.

Carter trotted to a row of pay phones, punched the area code for Washington, D.C., and keyed in the private code that would give him a secure line to Hawk's penthouse office above Amalgamated Press and Wire Services, a news bureau long used as AXE's cover organization. Although AXE used it as a convenient front, it operated at a profit. Hawk liked success in all things.

The news service also gave Hawk a constant stream of information. He lived in front of his news monitors, fax machines, computer screens, and telexes, assuring him of the fast-breaking news he required to run AXE, as well as providing him an excuse to avoid personal human contact.

Reaching into his breast wallet for a special shielding device, Carter fit three sheets of titanium-coated lead together into a small tent that covered the buttons of the telephone. He punched in the numbers of Hawk's private line.

Suddenly a huge explosion thundered in the air. A roll of deafening sound, debris, and hot air swept over Carter like a tidal wave.

He grabbed the telephone stand, hunched over, and shielded his face. Concrete chips stung the back of his neck. Was it one explosion, or two? If it was two, they were very close together.

He turned. The elegant Star of India restaurant had partially collapsed. Clouds of dust and smoke billowed above it. Wood creaked, and a sagging corner swayed and dropped another foot. The stucco exterior crumbled in spots, revealing the steel mesh supports beneath. All the windows were blown out. A toppled tree had crushed a white limousine parked close to the side. The air stank of fire and death.

Since the noise was deafening and the damage extensive, immediately Carter thought that it was most likely the result of high-powered gelignite.

"What's up, Nick?" David Hawk's voice suddenly came over the line between Dallas and Washington. "You're early."

"I'm also grateful," Carter said. "Your tip saved my life."

"Are you saying someone recognized you and tried to kill you?"

"I was tracking Perrine as per instructions, sir."

Carter heard the click of a cigarette lighter and knew that Hawk had fired up one of his foul-smelling cigars.

"I'd followed him to a restaurant. The Star of India. Very expensive, and the cuisine is excellent. Bruce Campbell was already there."

"Bruce Campbell? The assassin?"

"Yes, sir. And Campbell was there on business. I watched him prepare a blowgun. He didn't notice me. He was studying Perrine."

"Ah, yes," Hawk said with satisfaction. "It all comes 'round. Perrine was the target."

"Then a gorgeous brunette had a fight with her boy friend. She threw her drink at him and stalked out, right past my table."

"A great temptation for you, I'm sure. And then . . . ?"

"She told me to contact a cigar-smoking friend from an outside telephone."

Hawk was silent. "Possibly a ruse to get my number with one of those blasted high-tech gadgets."

"I thought of that, sir, and took precautions."

"I didn't send her, Nick. Why did she want to get you out of there? Has something else happened?"

"The restaurant was bombed," Carter said simply. "In fact, it exploded just before you came on the line. A thoroughly professional job, very nasty. Obviously planned to inflict the most damage to property and personnel."

"We need to see what's going on there. Perrine or Campbell may have had vital information about a mess that's breaking. Can you get back inside?"

Carter looked at the billowing smoke, the small, intense fires, the great piles of debris, and everywhere things hanging from walls and ceilings like shedding skin after a bad sunburn.

"I'll get in," Carter said.

"Good. See if you can search Perrine. Campbell bought it in there?"

"Probably, sir. It was a heavy blast. There couldn't be many survivors."

"Search Campbell, too. This is beginning to make sense."

Hawk was silent, thinking. Carter listened as Hawk noisily inhaled and exhaled in the distance.

"That's the connection," Hawk muttered at last, talking to himself. "Yes. I'm sure of it."

Again a pause as the AXE chief gusted in more of his noxious cigar. In his mind, Carter could smell its stench. It was one of those odors you never forgot. All part of the Hawk legend.

"Nick, there's a microdot that either Campbell or Perrine might have," David Hawk said abruptly. "Also a small Sanskrit scroll. The microdot is more important, but the scroll could be enormously helpful. It's about six inches long. Perrine was probably carrying it, but either might have it. Get back in there quickly, before the police. Find the microdot and the scroll. Any questions?"

"I assume you had nothing to do with the brunette?"

"Beautiful women are your department," Hawk chuckled.

"But she knew about me—and you."

"Ah, yes." Hawk pumped on his cigar, the sound echoing hollowly over the long distance. "But this is the

first I've heard of her. Now, get back in there." The line
went dead.

Nick Carter hurried back across the parking lot toward
the naked framework that had so recently been a beautiful
restaurant. Stucco was still crumbling off, forming white
snowy piles around the exterior.

Carter strode into what had been the foyer. The maître d'
was dead on the floor, a bloody gash on his head.
Carter took a deep breath. The carnage was going to be
terrible.

He moved on past a rubble of plaster, velvet drapes,
shards of glass, and the corpses. Occasional tongues of
flame licked at cloth and bits of wood. Faint voices called
for help, dazed by pain and the suddenness of shock. Three
automatic sprinklers trickled desultory sprays of water.
Smoke coiled, clouding the air. There was a nose-stinging
smell of burned wood, fabric, flesh.

In the distance, fire truck and police sirens screamed.

As Carter made his way to the area where Campbell and
Perrine had been sitting, he saw that his own table was
smashed under a large beam.

Had he remained, he'd be dead.

He shook his head, sad, disgusted, growing angry.
Around him, a half-dozen survivors wandered about,
stunned.

He located Campbell's table, and the bearded assassin
sprawled over shattered chairs and torn tablecloths. Judging
from his open-mouthed gape and his frozen stare, the force
of the blast had killed him instantly.

Carter went to work, searching the body for microdots or
anything that might give Hawk information. The assassin
carried few things: an old silver money clip, a pocket knife,
a lacquered Tiffany lighter. His breast wallet had two credit
cards under other names and about a thousand dollars in
large bills.

At last the sirens screamed into the parking lot and
suddenly stopped. The silence was a relief. A woman with
gray hair and a tattered skirt burst into tears.

Carter pulled off one of Campbell's shoes; the blast had already removed the other. He stripped off the socks and checked for a microdot between the toes, a favorite place.

Three Dallas cops and two firemen stood frozen in the front doorway, then quickly moved in.

"Hey! What the hell're you doin'?" a Dallas cop asked.

"Checking for signs of life," Carter said as he worked over Campbell's other foot.

The reply seemed to satisfy the cop, who looked dazed himself at the tragic loss of life and the vast destruction. The cop moved on, caught a stunned, wandering survivor, and escorted him to the door.

More people arrived, including paramedics.

Carter abandoned Bruce Campbell's corpse and moved on to look for Perrine's. He dug beneath piles of shattered dishes, bent silverware, and chunks of ceiling plaster until he found a hand, then an arm, then the crushed chest.

But the blast had not killed Perrine. Campbell had managed that first.

Carter carefully removed Campbell's dart from Perrine's neck and hid it beneath his jacket collar. In the murdered man's pockets were over five thousand dollars secured in a diamond-studded money clip, a simple key ring, and an intricately carved morocco notebook the size of a matchbook. It had numbers and addresses. Carter pocketed it and pried off Perrine's two gold rings, looking inside for microdots.

"Hey!" a fireman yelled. "Watch out!"

People lifted their eyes, stared at him, then twisted their heads looking around fearfully for the next disaster.

The ceiling groaned and collapsed in a powdery spray of debris and dust. As it came down, the survivors and rescuers scattered.

Carter ducked and missed most of it. He tugged off Perrine's boots, peeled off his socks, and resumed the slow, deliberate process of search. He found nothing. He smashed the heels off both boots in case there was a hollowed-out compartment. Again, nothing. Perrine was clean.

Stripping the jacket from Perrine, Carter noticed that a portion of the industrialist's inner arm had been mutilated. As he tried to get a closer look, his hand touched something in the jacket sleeve that was solid, oddly solid. It didn't belong there. Something larger than a fountain pen.

Carter felt it, moved it around, and discovered it was located between the breast pocket and the lining of Perrine's jacket.

Carter flexed his right arm and Hugo, a razor-sharp stiletto sheathed in a chamois holster, sprang into his hand. He slit the lining and withdrew a leather pouch. Then he slit the pouch and shook into his hand a scroll about six inches long and perhaps an inch in diameter.

Carter slipped Hugo back into its sheath. He tugged the silken cords that tied the scroll. The writing surface was a pounded, woven material. Looking at the tightly clustered text, he recognized it as Sanskrit, the religious and scholarly language of Hindu India. He guessed from the style of the calligraphy and the condition of the writing surface that the scroll was ancient, perhaps a thousand years old.

A television news team appeared. Technicians set up equipment while reporters stuck microphones before anyone who walked by. A director shouted for the camera to pan the crowd and debris.

Swiftly, carefully, Carter rewound the scroll and tied it.

"Careful!" a woman's voice cried at his back. She could have been with the camera crew. She could have been part of any of the dozen emergency teams responding to the call at the Star of India. She could even have been warning Carter about some menace lurking behind him.

From the corner of his eye, Carter saw movement. It was unnatural, violent. He had an impression of a fireman's yellow slicker.

With the smooth, practiced speed of the trained agent, Carter spun on his heel.

Dressed in a fireman's slicker, a man swung an ax handle at Carter's skull.

Carter blocked with one arm, grabbed the "fireman's" other arm, and flipped him over on his back.

But as the man flipped over, he kicked high and struck Carter's neck. It stunned him for a moment.

Long enough for the guy to jump back onto his feet and this time crash the ax handle against Carter's head. Red and white pain streaked behind Carter's eyes.

Even as he was losing consciousness, Carter felt himself kick out and catch the guy in the knee. He heard a sharp intake of breath and a groan.

And then blackness enveloped Carter.

When at last he opened his eyes, he had no idea how much time had passed. Not long, he supposed, because the rescuers had not yet gotten around to him.

He lay there quietly a moment. His head throbbed, but it was a dull ache, not sharp, and he felt no dizziness. The guy had caught his head just right but hadn't inflicted any permanent damage.

And then he remembered: the Sanskrit scroll. He reached for it. Felt all around, sat up, still looking. It was gone!

He stood, searching quickly. The scroll was definitely gone.

Now a fireman stood next to Carter. "What about it, cowboy? Want some help getting out of this mess?"

Carter scanned him closely. He wore a white slicker with the distinctive Dallas city logo.

"Any of your group wear a yellow slicker?" Carter asked.

The fireman watched him as though he thought he might be in shock. He checked Carter's eyes. "Hmm. Pupils are okay. Maybe you did a little hallucinatin'. We all wear white slickers here in Dallas, cowboy. You from out of town?"

"Thanks. That's what I thought." Carter stood and dusted himself off. His head was feeling better, but he was going to have one hell of a bump. He touched the spot lightly, and winced. All part of the job, he thought ruefully.

"Hey there!" the fireman said, pointing to a figure hastily exiting through the rubble-filled entryway. "That guy's got a yellow slicker. What's goin' on?"

"Thanks!" Carter said and sped toward the entry.

TWO

Carter fought his way through the rubble and the growing number of people—survivors, rescuers, and the morbidly curious.

He moved on toward the foyer where beyond spread the parking lot. And then he saw it. The yellow slicker, lying crumpled in the doorway to the men's rest room.

The pockets contained lint and a book of matches. A small slip of paper had seven numbers scribbled on it. The digits looked like a telephone number. Carter pocketed it and tossed the yellow slicker back on the floor.

He ran to the parking lot.

Across the way, a red unmarked van pulled out of the lot and into the street. Carter took several great strides after it, hoping for a look at the license number, but he was too late.

He ran his fingers through his dark hair, straightened his clothes, and ordered himself to ignore the beginnings of a horrendous headache.

He wandered around the scene, watching bystanders and workers for anyone who reacted to his presence. Perhaps someone suddenly ducking behind another person, turning

too casually to face the opposite direction, or—panicked—
racing away. But no one stared at him or seemed interested
in him at all.

Police were setting up barriers and herding onlookers
away. New sirens screamed in the night and red lights
flashed as more ambulances and fire trucks roared up to the
noisy, busy throng. The Star of India disaster was worse
than they'd first believed.

Carter studied the crowd for the brunette. Again, no luck.
He wondered whether he'd met her before. She could be an
agent ordered to memorize his photo so she could contact
him. She had, obviously, purposefully saved him. Why?
And why had she then run away?

He moved quickly back to the smoldering restaurant,
shoving his way through crowds and flashing his meaning-
less but official-looking ID card at a cop standing at the
door.

Inside, firemen directed streams of water at burning spots
while paramedics and doctors identified the dead, ordered
their separation from the living, and—faces grim—treated
the few survivors.

What Carter sought—the maître d's stand—had been
blown across the room. He crouched by it, searching, and at
last found it: a thick reservation book with diagrams of the
table layout in the main dining room. Every table in the
restaurant was accounted for.

Carter identified his own table, *N. Carter*. He found the
table where *P. Perrine* had sat and the table where Bruce
Campbell had been. The assassin had given an assumed
name, *R. Kipling*. Carter had known of Campbell's activities for nearly two years and had always supposed Campbell
was a pseudonym. "R. Kipling" indicated a literary sense
of humor Carter found surprising in an international killer.

He traced the table where the brunette had sat with her
date. Carter saw immediately that he had a break. The name
was *G. Houghton*. That should be easy to check. How many
could there be in the telephone book, even in Dallas?

A hand reached for the reservation book.

"That will make a great evening news feature," said a chesty blonde with a Channel Three blazer. "There were some kids celebrating graduation and at least two wedding anniversaries here tonight." She gave Carter a frank smile. "I'd be very grateful if I could have this."

"You ever hear of sensitive reporting?" Carter growled, disgusted.

A cop stepped forward and reached for the book. "It's our only clue about the bodies—and the parts. Your story can wait, lady."

"The public has a right to know," she said indignantly, and by rote. "This is a major disaster."

"The friends and relatives of the survivors have rights too," the cop snapped.

Carter tossed the reservation book to the cop.

"Hey!" she said, disappointed.

Carter left. On the curb he hailed a cab and told the driver to stop at the first phone booth.

After several no answers, dead ends, and busy signals, he finally reached a maid who identified G. Houghton as George Houghton III, an investment counselor, who was out that evening with a new client.

"Her name?" Carter asked.

"Que?" she said.

The maid's English was limited. Carter switched to Spanish, and soon was invited to George Houghton's luxurious condo in Preston Oaks, a tree-lined, elite section of Dallas. He arrived a half hour later.

At first the maid said she thought Mr. Houghton would be upset if she gave him too much information, and so Carter had to explain to her that Mr. Houghton's concerns no longer had anything to do with worldly matters.

The maid crossed herself. *"Muerto?"* she repeated in Spanish. "Señor Houghton is really dead? Aiee! Poor man!"

She led Carter to a large, professionally decorated room that served as Houghton's home office. Very ballsy and masculine, he observed, with framed hunting lithographs, hand-carved duck decoys, a rack of custom shotguns, and framed color photos.

"Señor Houghton," the maid said, pointing to the photos.

Houghton was a thin man with a round belly from too much self-indulgence. In one photo he was wearing tennis togs and trying to look as if he had a fierce serve.

Carter went to Houghton's desk and opened drawers.

The maid whimpered, then wept. "Ohhh, what will I do?" she cried. Tears streamed down her face as she stared accusingly at Carter. "I have no money! And now I have no job!" She fell onto the leather sofa and cried harder.

"I'm sorry," Carter said, genuinely touched. "I can give you some money. Not a lot, but maybe enough to tide you over until you can find another job."

"Asshole!" she shouted, pounding the sofa while more tears rolled down her reddened cheeks. "Gringo creep. Pervert!"

It took Carter a moment to realize she was referring to George Houghton. This was an interesting development. He moved to the sofa and pressed five hundred dollars into her palm.

"Here," he said gently. "I really am sorry. I hope this will help."

She was a tiny woman in her twenties, small but curvy. Especially attractive round breasts. Her uniform was fairly conventional except that as Carter leaned over he caught a glimpse of some expensive black frill across the cleavage that made him suspicious.

"*Gracias,*" she whimpered. She clutched the money to her breast. It heaved nicely. "*Muchas gracias.*" She looked at Carter as if he were her savior.

"He told me he was going to send me to night school," she said. She sniffled, and her eyes narrowed. "But he never got around to it," she said bitterly. "He said he had . . . better . . . things . . . for me to do." She paused meaningfully. "You know what I mean?"

"He was your lover?"

"Love had nothing to do with it! He was a pig! A glutton! He *used* me!" Again she broke out into tears.

"I understand." He patted her shoulder. "If I find out anything that can help you, I'll get back to you. How can I reach you?"

She told him her telephone number and he jotted it down. Carter figured he probably wouldn't need to talk to her again, and it was even less likely that he would find something about Houghton that would help her, but he believed in being thorough. You couldn't survive in his business if you weren't.

Carter finished searching the office. He found two important items: a client list and a date book. For tonight, written in the erect, stiff script of Houghton's other entries was: *L. Chatterjee. Drinks, 7:00. Dinner, 8:00. Star of India*.

There was no address for L. Chatterjee, only the hand-written designation *TC* and a phone number.

Carter called a special AXE number to get the code number for Dallas that would cause the phone company to give him an address if only the phone number were known.

The initials TC turned out to be a posh section of Dallas—Turtle Creek. Half an hour later, Carter was there, dropped off by taxi at the elegant wrought-iron guard gate to a sumptuous complex of condos.

He pressed the button next to L. Chatterjee.

"Yes?" said the slightly distorted female voice through the speaker phone next to the resident roster. "What do you want?"

"Security force, ma'am."

There was a long pause, then L. Chatterjee decided: "Bullshit. You are not from security. Who the hell are you? What do you want?" There was a short hesitation. When she spoke again, there was resignation in her voice. "It's Carter, isn't it? Dammit. You have found me already."

A buzzer sounded, and the wrought-iron gate swung silently open.

Carter followed a path that wound past parklike gardens,

riding trails, and championship tennis courts on which the
luxury condos fronted.

At last he saw her, framed in an open doorway on the
second floor.

"I figured you would probably track me down," she said.
She gestured him up the tiled stairs. "I just didn't think it
would be so soon." She wore a heavy white terry-cloth robe
and a large towel wrapped like a turban around her head.
There was the warm smell of roses about her.

He studied her. "I just wanted to thank you for your tip,
Ms. Chatterjee."

"Call me Lalita," she told him. She led him into her
condo and motioned him to a large, overstuffed sofa.

"I think you owe me an explanation."

He sat. His eyes took in the small room. Its walls and
surfaces were crammed with Indian art and artifacts—
drawings, paintings, metalwork, bronze, statues, carved
wooden animals. It had the feel of a museum, as if no one
lived here. It made him wonder whether this wasn't her
principal dwelling, whether she kept other similar small
residences in other cities.

"I have no explanation," she said, and sat across from
him in a big easy chair. "At least none that I can give you."

He considered her. There was an air of ripe beauty about
her, as if she had reached her prime, but that it would
continue for years. Some women were like that, wearing
well. Others peaked suddenly and headed downhill instantly. He'd long thought the difference had to do with
character. He suspected Lalita Chatterjee had that old-
fashioned quality called character.

"Then tell me about yourself," he suggested.

"I was born in India, but most of my education was here
and in Europe. I put some time in at Berkeley and the
London School of Economics."

"A Communist?" Carter said.

She waved away the question. "I just saved your life, you
know. Show some respect. Of course I'm not a Commu-

nist." She pulled her robe more closely around her, as if she had a chill.

He nodded, accepted her word. "Go on."

"I'm from a family and a group that are very well connected in India. India is a diverse nation in some ways, with many different ideologies. In other ways, we Indians are all the same."

"Is it part of your culture to abandon someone to die?"

"What?" She didn't understand.

"You knew that the Star of India was going to be bombed, right down to the minute it happened. Yet you walked out on George Houghton, left him to be killed. Just as you left *everyone* in the restaurant to be killed. Except me."

Lalita Chatterjee held up a hand. "I cannot tell you why I have done what I have done. I am what I am, and I have obligations you know nothing about. Obligations you can know nothing about. Probably ever. As for George, he was blind drunk and refused to come with me when I tried to get him out of there." She paused. "I will also add that I found out about the *possibility* of a bomb only minutes before I spoke to you."

She stood, tall and regal, and went to a small liquor cabinet. She poured two fingers of brandy and knocked it back in one gulp.

"What a terrible day," she muttered.

Carter studied the collection of Indian art in her colorful living room. "You're Hindu, aren't you?"

Her eyes met him with frank appraisal. "Observant, aren't you?"

"The Star of India is Pakistani, which means a Muslim influence. What were you doing in a restaurant where the atmosphere and culture were at odds with your own preferences?"

"I was doing the same thing in the Star of India you were, Nick Carter. I was working."

"For your country?"

"For my beliefs. I thought your own beliefs were such that the world would be better off with you still alive."

"That's why you saved me?"

She nodded.

"I do a job," Carter said. "Obviously you know what it is."

Lalita Chatterjee shook her head. "Men are so vain. The fact that I—a mere woman—know about you and your cigar-smoking David Hawk causes you to think there was some security leak and you are already worried where it can be. Even the fact that someone knows enough about you to save your life somehow leaves you feeling compromised. The truth is, Nick Carter, I saw you at a reception given reluctantly by David Hawk some three years ago. I was told then who you are. Of course, I'd already heard of you. There is no security leak. Like you, I am good at what I do."

"I believe that," Carter said. "How did you find me?"

"I saw you trailing Perrine."

"Why was there a contract on him?"

"He was known to have extensive trade with Pakistan, and to have used his contacts there to transfer arms, ammunition, jet fighters, and heat-seeking rockets to causes that are not among the most popular."

"Ahh," Carter said, understanding.

"He had a great many ties with the Central Intelligence Agency, directly and as a consultant to many of the CIA's front organizations." She spread her hands. "It could be a customer he cheated. A rival. A government agency he refused to sell to. Someone he double-crossed. Or anyone who has a strong aversion to covert activities or to the profiteering on the sales of arms to nonspecific political causes. Perrine was popular with some, hated by many."

"Do you have a strong aversion to such activities?"

"I am in favor of the orderly commerce between nations and people. They do not always have to love one another as brother and sister, but they should show respect, and certainly not resort to the mass murder we saw at the restaurant tonight."

"I'd come to the conclusion that the Star of India was a sort of free port, a front for Pakistani groups who were moving arms and technology to countries and groups that might not be willing or able to compete in the open market."

She nodded for him to continue.

"It might even be discovered that some of the guests and employees had direct and indirect connections to Langley, Virginia."

"Very good indeed, Carter. That is information that is held only by a handful of CIA operatives, members of the State Department, and, of course, by select members of the intelligence community."

"Such as ourselves?" Carter said.

Lalita Chatterjee met the challenge. "If you are trying to imply that I have guilty knowledge because I am a Hindu and I had dinner in a Muslim restaurant where bombs exploded—"

"Interesting that you use the plural," Carter cut in. "Bombs, not a bomb. I thought there were two closely timed explosions, but then, I was closer than you."

"If you are looking for possible causes or nations to blame," she said, "I can suggest your CIA, Libya, South Africa, the Sikh nation, South Korea, North Korea, Iraq, Iran, the Irish Republican Army, and even Taiwan as highly probable suspects."

"What about your country?"

"India?" She laughed. "Yes, it is always wise to consider the unthinkable about India."

Carter waited.

"Your superiors had you watching a place that had become a hot spot," she said. "What would the United States public at large think if they knew how many guns, planes, rockets, even chemical warfare weapons were traded on such a covert marketplace? It makes sense that you are watching for trends, danger signs."

"Does that mean your people are having you watched for danger signs?"

"Ah!" Lalita Chatterjee nodded. "Now you are beginning to ask questions worthy of Nick Carter. With so many people in India, so many factions, so much poverty, so many different languages, so many different gods and goddesses to worship, so much illiteracy, there is always the danger of a new faction, a new cult, formed by idealists who are ready to take dramatic action—"

"—and perhaps even die for their idealism?"

"There is an expression in my country, 'Give me blood and I will give you freedom.' It was last used by Gandhi and the followers of his philosophy of nonviolence. Odd as it may seem, the nonviolent among us are equally ready to die for their beliefs."

"And so you are beginning to see certain trends, much as I saw trends about the Star of India restaurant."

"Yes, exactly, Carter. I see a resurgence of nationalist pride, pride in the old heritage and glory of India. As you know, India is an ancient civilization."

"Before the Raj and the British?"

"Long before the British."

Carter fingered the bump on the back of his head. "After the explosion tonight, I went back inside, looking for things. I briefly had in my possession a small scroll. It was written in Sanskrit—"

"It is said that Sanskrit is first the language of God, then the language of the scholar."

"Someone whacked me with an ax handle and relieved me of the language of God and the scholar. From what little I got to see of the scroll, it was maybe a thousand years old, give or take, and it spoke of a man who was a soldier but no longer had the taste for battle."

"You were able to read it?" she asked, unable to mask her surprise.

"The light was awful and there was a lot going on."

Lalita Chatterjee shook her head impatiently. "I don't care about that. I'm asking if you know Sanskrit."

Carter nodded.

"Amazing!" Lalita Chatterjee said. "You are a remarkable man, Carter."

"Ah," he said, amused. "I have your respect."

"Of course," she said sincerely. "Sanskrit is so refined. Ever so much more difficult than even Latin— And the notion that you, a Westerner—"

Carter laughed. "Glad I could surprise you. We Westerners do know a few things."

"I'm sorry." Lalita Chatterjee stood, approached Carter. "I didn't mean to insult you. Of course I have heard so many things about the great Nick Carter."

She touched his wrist, allowed her fingers to linger, soothing and suggestive. He took her hand, kissed the back, the palm. Her eyes flashed. A slight flush rose up her throat. He stood. The exotic rose scent of her filled his senses.

He circled an arm around her waist, pulled her close.

"I already know one bit of wisdom that will be important to both of us," she whispered. She reached behind him and brought up to eye level a hand-sewn manuscript with Sanskrit lettered on the cover. "Do you recognize this, Mr. Nick Carter?"

Carter glanced at it, then his gaze returned to focus on her magnificent dark eyes. "Should I?" Beneath his arms the equally magnificent hips moved.

"It's written by a scholar named Vatsyayana—"

"Of course," he said, smiling broadly. He knew now what she held, and why she thought it important. "It's the *Kama Sutra*, the great Hindu treatise on lovemaking."

It was her turn to smile deeply into his eyes. "Yes," she said, "the art of the ways in which men and women may give each other the most exquisite pleasures. Sexual pleasures. It is already a good sign that you are aware of it. I hope you had nothing else planned for tonight."

"Nothing at all," Carter said, "except the wisdom that awaits us."

He kissed her, and she moved lithe and demanding in his arms.

THREE

Nick Carter followed Lalita Chatterjee to her tiny outdoor patio beneath the vast Texas night.

The patio was completely enclosed in glass. Above them the high canopy of diamond-bright stars sparkled and blushed. City lights spread in an ocean of twinkling lights. Embedded in the patio was a steaming hot tub, waiting for them.

"Now this," Lalita announced, slipping her smooth cool hands up Carter's chest, beneath his jacket. She pulled it down off his shoulders and tossed it on a canvas chair. "And this." The cool hands pulled off his bolo tie, efficiently unbuttoned his shirt, ran up from his belly and over his chest to his shoulders. "Such shoulders," she murmured. "Marvelous." She pulled off his shirt, went for his belt buckle.

"No," he told her, even though the heat spread insistent from his groin. "You now."

He untied her sash's knot, and the robe swung open to reveal round pink breasts, a smooth flat belly.

"Oh!" she said, and caught her breath as the steamy air

hit her skin. "You're too fast!" she said, retying her belt with nimble fingers. "Much too fast!"

He laughed, the sight of her nudity fresh in his mind. He sat on the canvas chair and shucked off his lizard-skin boots. She knelt in front of him and undid his pants.

"Such a man!"

He reached for her.

She slipped away. "But such impatience!" She went to the door. "Get into the tub. I'll be right back."

He finished undressing, calmed himself. He stood for a moment at the edge of the tub, then stepped in. He sank into the warm water and felt the tension dissolve in his shoulders and back. He wondered what she had in mind. At this point he didn't much care about the details. Whatever it was, he expected it would be satisfying. One way or the other.

He leaned to the side, turned on a switch, and Jacuzzi jets stirred the water into a froth. He moved so the pounding jets could massage his back.

Soon Lalita returned carrying a tray. She knelt, her breasts rising sensually between the deep collar of her robe, and set the tray beside the tub. On it was iced tea, filled with crushed mint leaves.

"You see, I came back," she said, and poured the contents of a large pitcher into the tub.

"Thought you would," he said.

"Ah, you trust me then."

"*Want* to trust is closer."

"No," she smilingly corrected him. "Just plain *want*, I imagine. As I do you."

He reached a wet hand up under the robe. She shivered delicately. He felt his need build. Waves of a perfumed substance that had come from the pitcher—part rose, part violet—began to suffuse the water.

"This is right out of the *Kama Sutra*," he said.

"Ah, yes."

She stood unmoving for a moment, enjoying his hands. Then she untied the belt of her terry-cloth robe and let it fall from her shoulders. The white robe framed her slender beauty and the glowing almond color of her skin.

In one smooth motion she pulled the towel from her head and her long dark hair cascaded down and around her shoulders.

In all this her movements were precise, timed. She was going through a ritual, doing everything according to plan. She was establishing a mood.

This amused him. He grabbed her hand, tugged, and brought her yelping with surprise into the tub on top of him. Their bodies entwined immediately, automatically.

Her legs encircled him and her hands probed, looking for places that would cause him to respond excitedly.

At the same time, Carter ran his fingers over her sleek firmness, felt the velvety skin, the long curves, the perfect smooth planes. She turned and responded languidly, then with greater intensity, an instrument to his music.

Then she stiffened, resisted. She was trying to gain control. She moved her hands along his inner thighs, up and down, producing delicious sensations.

The excitement grew and Carter pulled her on top of him, her hips over his . . .

"Dammit, Nick!" she complained. "How can I do the Expanding Lotus for us if you keep breaking the concentration?"

"Too late," Carter said, pressing against her, rubbing with an intensity that drove her to agitation.

She arched her back and thrust against him. "No patience, Nick. The riches of the ages . . . the force of mounting fulfillment—"

Carter held on and she arched back, closed her eyes, and dug her nails into his back. She moaned softly, then with greater intensity until she peaked and cried out.

"It looks like the riches of the ages are right here," Carter said, smiling, as he relaxed in the warm water.

"There is ever so much more with discipline," she panted, recovering. "Things that can be experienced through the *chakras*. Why must Westerners be so eager for the obvious results?"

Carter got to his knees, swung out of the tub, reached in, and pulled Lalita Chatterjee up toward him.

"Okay," he said, "let's try it your way."

"But we're all wet!" she protested. "We need to be dried or oiled."

Carter yanked a large bath sheet from the rack and toweled her dry.

"I believe in spontaneity," he said.

"Not like that!" she said. "You're getting me excited again. How can we do the old ways of the sages if you keep getting horny and breaking concentration?"

Carter laughed.

He picked up Lalita Chatterjee and carried her into the bedroom. He flicked on the light. Small and simple, the room had bright Madras curtains, a few large plants, a large stone sculpture, and colorful miniature paintings that appeared to be quite old.

He sat her down on the bed, eased down next to her, and drew her to him in a long embrace.

"Here we are," he said, breathing in her ear. "We'll try it your way."

She turned to study him, considering.

"Yes," she said, "this is how we'll do it."

She patted a place for him on the edge of the bed. Obediently Carter landed there.

"I don't like that smile on your face. You've got to take this seriously, Nick. Now, relax!"

"How can I relax with you doing that so suggestively?"

"Close your eyes and try not to think about what I'm doing."

"All right. Weird, but all right."

Carter closed his eyes, felt one of her legs drape over him, then a slight pressure between his legs. Very nice. Ahhh. He gave in to the pressure.

"Perfect," she decided. "Now give me your hand."

Carter felt his hand close over the velvet firmness of her

breast. He kneaded slowly, aware of the effect it was having on her.

"Almost there, Nick. This is a dandy one."

She shifted her weight, and suddenly they were merged.

"Careful how you move," she said, "this gets very sensitive."

But she was too late with her warning.

The heightened sensitivity made Carter move with a forward thrust that caused a long, low moan to escape from her throat. In a moment she was moving rhythmically against her.

"Dammit, Nick, we're going too fast!"

But Carter noticed that she was the one doing the thrusting and moving. Then spasms wracked her body. And then Carter thought what the hell, why not. He moved quickly, enjoying the close and intense sense of intimacy until she thrust one more time to her explosion.

"Oh, Nick," she sighed, breathing hard. She shuddered, limp in his arms. "We're not getting it right and we don't have much time."

Carter rolled her over on her back, stroking the area under her throat.

"Seems to me we've been getting it right," he murmured.

She propped herself up on one elbow. "You know what I mean. The old ways. The *Kama Sutra*."

"Ah," Carter said. "Yes." He moved his face to the inviting cleft between her breasts.

"That's the way," she urged. "It should be more like a ritual. A celebration. Use your imagination."

Carter inhaled the warm musk of her body, the heady scent of roses. He felt himself move against her.

"You have no discipline," Lalita Chatterjee said.

"No, but I have what I want." His breath was ragged. "You."

She was on top of him suddenly, thrusting, moving with complete abandon. He felt his own need rise, grow, demand . . . until, sweating and breathless, they exploded together, their bodies wracked in shudders.

Afterward, they lay arms wrapped around one another, breathing peacefully.

After a few moments she began to laugh. "I don't know if we'll ever get around to the old stuff, Nick, but I'm willing to settle for what we've got."

"That's good," Carter said sleepily. "I told you spontaneity has its advantages."

In an hour Carter left to check on the possibility that he'd picked up a tail at Lalita Chatterjee's. But he was still clean, and he ordered the taxi driver to take him to a large shopping mall where he used the randomness of a large bank of phones to ensure privacy.

David Hawk, crusty, short-tempered, answered on the second ring.

"It's jelling into something of major significance involving India, Nick." He drew on his cigar. "Pieces are starting to fall together. A curator of Indian artifacts was murdered at the Los Angeles Museum of Art while setting up an exhibit."

"A big exhibit, sir?"

"Major. Hundreds of ancient pieces. Then we have the bombing at the Star of India, the bloody massacre there, and early today I heard about another incident that happened some time ago. It's being kept very quiet by the victims."

"Yes, sir." Carter listened as Hawk puffed noisily.

"There was an incident at the Prince Alphonse Museum in Madrid. A bombing. Just before the opening of a large new exhibit. The people there are all nonpolitical sorts. Their biggest worry is that if word leaks out, no more private collectors will be willing to lend them significant works of art and, of course, no donations will roll in from their wealthy patrons."

"Do we know what kind of exhibit it was?"

"Damned right we do. 'The Heritage of India'!"

"Hindu or Muslim art, sir?"

"What?" Hawk thought for a moment. He smoked.

"Good question. I'll find out. Better still, *you* find out. See whether it means anything. Go to Madrid."

Carter gave Hawk a brief rundown of his conversation with Lalita Chatterjee and her conviction that there was a sudden resurgence of old-style nationalist pride in Hindu India.

"A lot of splinter groups," Carter added, "are all willing to go to extremes."

"That could be it," Hawk agreed. "Something like the Sikhs, demanding to establish their particular version of justice. A breeding ground for some organization wanting to bring the world to a screeching halt and drag it back into the past. Power and politics, Nick. Check it out."

Somehow David Hawk managed to inhale and end the conversation before Carter could respond.

Carter hung up and went to another pay phone and dialed Lalita Chatterjee.

"This call is secured with a scrambler," he told her.

"Couldn't stay away, eh, Nick?" There was mischief in her voice.

"This is about work, Lalita. What do you know about the Prince Alphonse Museum in Madrid?"

He could feel a tangible jab of surprise from her. "My, my. But you do move quickly."

"The advantages of a small organization. What's going on in Madrid, Lalita?"

"All right. Yes. Well, I suppose it wouldn't hurt to tell you. We know so little anyway, but you must promise me this won't go to any other agencies. A real promise."

"You've got my word," Carter said.

"There was to have been a major exhibition given heavy backing by the Spanish and Indian governments. It was interrupted."

"Interrupted? How?"

"Terrorism. Guns, bombs, threats."

"How was this terrorism covered up?"

There was an edge of irony to Lalita Chatterjee's voice. "It cost a good deal of money and future favors."

"You don't sound as if you approve."

"I hardly had a choice. You know how that goes."

"I need a lead, Lalita."

"You're going to Madrid?"

"Right now."

"I should insist you come here first."

"Think about future favors instead, Lalita."

"You are the kind of professional I could work with. AXE is fortunate to have you. All right, Carter, here is your lead. When you go to Madrid and the Prince Alphonse, you should see Manuela Torres, the curator. She is an expert on Indian art and artifacts."

"Will she talk frankly? Can she be trusted?"

"She is absolutely trustworthy, although I am under an obligation to keep private where her basic loyalties lie. You are a quick study. You may discover that information yourself. In any case, mention my name. That should get you an opportunity."

"Thanks. Is there anything I should watch out for?" Carter asked.

"Oh, yes. Indeed." Her voice took on ominous, worried tones. "After you go to Madrid, you will undoubtedly want to go to India. So my message is that you should look out for all of India. Nothing there is as it seems. Keep your senses as sharp as you possibly can. Often what you see is not real, and what you can't see, is."

Carter made one more phone call to a favored travel agency in Georgetown.

He hailed a taxi and climbed into the back seat.

"The airport," he told the driver and closed the door. "There's an extra fifty bucks in it for you if you make it fast. I've got a flight to Washington that leaves in twenty minutes."

FOUR

Madrid, the ancient capital of Castile that had suffered through so many deadly struggles over the centuries, from the cymbal-clashing Moorish invaders and conquerors of the seventh century to the strutting Falangists of Generalissimo Francisco Franco only fifty years ago, lay like a jewel in the sun on its high plateau as Carter's jet settled for its landing. Huge Bernabeau Stadium, modern housing complexes, and man-made beaches spread out below, hiding much of the city's historic heritage.

Broad avenues, green promenades, and great parks filled with flowers marked the newer areas of urban development, but in Madrid there was no way to escape the past. Carter could see the Royal Casa de la Pandera built in 1672, the wooden dome of San Placido church, the huge dome of San Francisco el Grande, and the narrow streets and hidden alleys of the old section as the jet swept into the airport west of the city.

He passed through customs without incident, picked up his bag at the carousel—an AXE staffer had met him at the airport in Washington with a packed suitcase before Carter boarded his flight to Spain—and retrieved Hugo, Pierre, and Wilhelmina from the secret shielded compartments inside that had been developed by AXE's experts. In a taxi, he gave as his destination the Prince Alphonse Museum and settled back to enjoy the drive into the city. The cab raced in through the Plaza de Roma and along the Calle de Alcala with its rows of elegant shops to Puerta del Sol, the square that was the old heart of the city. From the Calle Mayor the cabbie turned into Calle de Bailen, went past the imposing Royal Palace, and pulled to a triumphant stop in front of what appeared to be an elegant restaurant: the Alphonse IV.

"Not a restaurant," Carter said with a laugh. "A museum. The Prince Alphonse. It should be an art museum."

The driver slapped his head. "Ah, *sí*, a thousand pardons, señor."

He was off again, backtracking along the magnificent Gran Via to Plaza de la Cibeles and Paseo del Prado and a screeching halt before the great Museo del Prado.

"The Prado is a fine art museum," Carter said dryly, "but it is not the Prince Alphonse. Maybe you'd better look in your guidebook."

Sullenly, the driver thumbed through his worn city guide. A Spaniard hates to have to look up anything, and a Madrid cab driver was ten times worse. He waved the book almost with joy: no Prince Alphonse Museum was listed.

"The American is wrong. There is no such crazy museum!"

Carter paid him, got out, and hailed another taxi. This driver took him all through the fine residential sections of Castellana and Recoletos and stopped with diminishing pride at five separate small museums, none named the Prince Alphonse. At the last, the second driver declared that the Yankee was a fool and a despicable person and should instantly get out of his taxi or fight him then and there.

Carter informed the fiery driver that if he wished to keep his ears he would instantly drive to a library and there Carter might get out and might pay him if he refrained from saying one more word. The driver drove to a large library. Carter

paid him the exact fare and left with a string of the best
Castilian curses following him.

But the library proved no more helpful: there was no
Prince Alphonse Museum listed in any reference book on
Madrid. There was only one good possibility left. He found
a telephone and called the American embassy.

"Hey," he said in his most Ugly-American voice, "I just
got here in Madrid and have been trying to locate a fabulous
art museum I been told holds the greatest collection of
Indian and Asian art stuff, but no one seems to know where
the hell it is! What kind of crazy city is this anyway? Do *you*
know where the hell this Prince Alphonse Museum is?"

"Perhaps a guidebook, sir? That—"

"Hell, mister, I've got guidebooks comin' out my ears!
Now you go find someone around there knows where the
hell this damned museum is!"

"Just a moment, sir."

It was less than a moment. A cool, hard voice came on.

"You want to visit the Prince Alphonse Museum, Mr.—?"

"Margate. Joe Margate from El Paso, and you bet I want
to visit this museum. Now, who are you and where is it?"

"I'm Lieutenant Colonel Sobers, Mr. Margate, assistant
military attaché. The Prince Alphonse is a relatively new
museum and out of the way. It's at Fourteen Calle
Campesino, and I'd be glad to take you there myself—"

"No need, Colonel, but thanks. I'll see my good buddy
General Taylor hears about you."

In his third taxi, Carter sat back and watched the elegant
streets and open spaces pass. The Prince Alphonse was
new, had a very low profile, but there was more to its low
profile than just either newness or exclusiveness. Lieutenant
Colonel Sobers had been on the phone in an instant, had
known all about the elusive museum, and the military
attaché's interest wouldn't be in art. By definition, every
military attaché was a CIA contact if not an operative. The
Prince Alphonse sounded like a strange museum all the
way.

It turned out to be even stranger than that.

Number 14 Calle Campesino was a large building that looked like a warehouse on a back street on the edge of the ancient narrow streets of the old town. An alley ran behind it, complete with double loading dock and an exit on two streets. The dock gates seemed buttoned up unusually tight. In fact the whole building had no windows on the first two floors, and no apparent entry or exit except the front double doors.

There was no sign of any terrorist damage on the outside of the building.

Carter went in.

"*Sí, señor*. Can I perhaps help you?"

He was a small, smiling brown man in a Nehru suit, his hands clasped and his head bowed slightly forward in the humble manner of a clerk in Imperial India. The rigid rules and habits of centuries are not easily lost.

"If you can direct me to Manuela Torres, you can."

The small man was distressed. "Ah, señor, the curator sees one only by appointment. Perhaps if you—"

"Perhaps you could tell her Lalita Chatterjee sent me to her."

"Ah, indeed? A Miss Chatterjee? I do not recognize the name of my countrywoman. If you—"

"Miss Torres will recognize Miss Chatterjee's name."

The small man bowed, but his eyes were far from servile now. "Of course, señor. I shall present the name to the curator. If you will be so kind as to wait here."

Carter studied the large main room that seemed to occupy half the building. The sight was dazzling even to his Western eyes. The whole museum was a repository of Indian, Tibetan, and Southeast Asian artworks with a heavy emphasis on Hindu India. It was a magnificent display to be hidden away in such an out-of-the-way neighborhood.

And there was no sign of bomb or bullet damage inside. Had Hawk and Lalita Chatterjee both been hoodwinked?

As Carter wandered among the displays of statuary, embossed gold plates, scrolls, and ancient artifacts, he began to notice the names of sponsors listed under many of the objects. Familiar names: Justin Dart, Oliver North, General Richard Secord, Maxwell Taylor, and other prominent people of the conservative international hawk community in America. Other names were those of men the Killmaster knew as CIA agents and contacts.

The museum's holdings were primarily Hindu and Buddhist pieces, but the listed sponsors were a lot closer to the late Zia ul-Haq and Muslim Pakistan. Carter wondered if this odd contradiction could have anything to do with the recent bombings and attacks. The Star of India had been a restaurant run by Muslims; the curator shot down in Los Angeles had been a Hindu. Was there some kind of religious civil war going on centered on the art treasures of ancient India?

As he thought, Carter continued to wander around the vast room. There were few doors in the walls, no sign of the facilities for visitors museums usually have. Carter tried the closed doors. All were locked.

"Visitors are not permitted beyond the exhibit areas, señor."

The small Indian stood behind Carter, his no longer servile eyes more than a little suspicious.

"Sorry," Carter said with an embarrassed smile. "Looking for a rest room."

"We have private facilities for use on request. Are you in urgent need?"

There was an antagonism and even sarcasm in the man's voice now. The old rules and habits can be used to mask interior hidden changes too. Now that they had been dropped, the small Indian showed a hard and belligerent pride, even arrogance as he watched Carter.

"It can wait. Do I get to talk to Manuela Torres?"

"This way," the man said coldly.

Even the curator's office wasn't through one of the doors into the rest of the building, but was partitioned off in a corner at the rear of the large exhibit room. The now

imperious attendant opened the door, motioned Carter
inside, and stalked away without a word.

"Mr. Nick Carter, I presume?"

Behind her large desk in the elegant office, Manuela
Torres was tall, blond, blue-eyed, and broad-shouldered.
Either she had a lot of Teutonic on her mother's side, or she
was that rare Spaniard who reflected the entry into Spain of
the Goths and Vandals almost two thousand years ago.

"Lalita must have described me well," Carter said as he
took a seat in the Mies Barcelona chair facing the curator.

"She told me only your name, and your interest in Indian
art," the blonde said coolly. "I deduced your appearance
from the tone of her voice. Lalita has a definite preference
in the men she sleeps with, and you are exactly her taste."

Her manner was as cool and aloof as her distant Nordic
ancestors, with an edge of disdain for the tastes of Lalita
Chatterjee. She was dressed in a simple white linen suit and
pale blue blouse that showed off full breasts that were also
high and firm. The linen suit clung to elegant lean curves
and seemed to ripple with athletic muscles under it. Her
pale hair was swept up in a severe twist.

"Does that disappoint you?"

"It doesn't affect me one way or the other, Mr. Carter.
Now, just what can I do for you?"

Her slim hands tapped impatiently. On her neat, clean,
orderly desk there were no photographs or personal objects.
Only a large, superb terra-cotta statue of a dancing Shiva
that Carter knew instantly had to be at least as old as the
ninth century. Manuela Torres knew her Indian art. The
piece would have been the envy of any museum anywhere,
and she had it for her desk.

"You can tell me who planted the bomb, made the
shooting attack and threats that disrupted your opening and
why."

He watched a strange change come over the blond. A
change that made him instantly aware of the beauty and
passion hidden behind the cool, businesslike manner. Her
blue eyes flashed, and her nostrils flared. Something about

what he had said had made her suddenly interested in him as
a man. She tried to disguise the sensual reaction as anger.

"You're not interested in art. Lalita lied to me. What are
you? CIA checking up on me? KGB? Mossad? I should
have known who Lalita would send. I've suspected her of
being more than a rich art amateur for a long time."

"What do you suspect she is?"

"Never mind!" She was on her feet, taller and slimmer
than Carter had realized. Her anger, or the passion he
couldn't yet place, made her tremble. "There is nothing I
can tell you because I know nothing. People who did not
want the exhibit to open tried to prevent it. That is all I
know."

Carter stood quickly, was close to her, their bodies almost
touching before she realized he had moved. He took her
hand. A violent shudder went through her, but she did not
pull away. Her eyes stared into his.

"Then I'll tell you," the Killmaster said, so close her
breath warmed his face. "This museum is a front, probably
for the CIA and private American interests supplying the
Pakistanis, Afghans, and all the other countries and con-
flicts the U.S. wants to aid but doesn't want the fact
broadcast. Whoever planted the bomb and disrupted your
opening are people who oppose the CIA or one or more of
the groups or countries it aids with the weapons, equipment,
and even hostages it routes through places like the Star of
India in Dallas and here. The question is, exactly who do
they oppose and who are they?"

They stared at each other, almost nose to nose. Manuela
Torres's eyes were wide. "Who are you?"

"I can't tell you that."

"You're a spy, aren't you? Bigger than the CIA, more
important."

"Let's say different," Carter said.

She moved close and seemed to collapse against the
Killmaster. "Yes, you're right. I have three degrees, have
studied in India, know as much about the art of the Orient
as anyone." She looked up, a hot need in her eyes. "But I

have no power. My knowledge means nothing. People like you have the power. The CIA. The power is in action, not in knowledge. I hate what I'm doing here. I count for nothing."

Carter realized she was one of those people who needed to feel a sense of power and so come to worship power. As a woman it took the form of being aroused by men with power. By kings, soldiers, diplomats, politicians, spies. It was something he could use. He held her hard by both arms and stared down at her.

"Then the museum *is* a front. A warehouse for arms, even nuclear warheads?"

She nodded. "Yes. The other half of the building is used by the CIA. Everything is shipped in and out disguised as art. I was offered the job of curator, paid well, and allowed to operate a fine museum, on the condition I hear and see nothing going on."

"Who made the attack on the museum?"

She shook her head. "I don't know, Mr. Carter."

"Nick," he said, and touched her soft face with one hand.

She shivered. "Nick. I can only think it must have been those opposed to the CIA, to Pakistan, to the Afghans. The Soviet Union, China, perhaps India itself."

"Lalita denies it could be India."

She curled her lip. "Lalita works for India. I've long suspected she is part of the Indian secret service."

Which would explain how Lalita Chatterjee knew when the Star of India was to be bombed. Especially if Indian agents had done the job. Carter was thinking about this when he became aware of Manuela Torres's arms around his neck.

"Come home with me, Nick. I can't think here. Come home with me now and perhaps I will remember more of what you want to know. I will tell you about Lalita Chatterjee, and give you more than she ever could."

Sometimes, Carter had to admit, his work could be more than pleasant. He smiled down at the intense blonde.

"I'm sure you will," he said.

FIVE

Pale where Lalita Chatterjee was dark, hot where the Indian devotee of the *Kama Sutra* was cool, Manuela Torres had never heard of the pleasures of holding back. The lean blonde made love with the fierceness of her distant Goth ancestors and the abandon of her Spanish heritage.

Bathed in sweat, Carter lay in the warm room with the shades drawn, battling an urge to sleep, his tanned skin glistening beside her long drenched body. He fought the weariness as he had so many times. There was a threat to the interests of world peace to be found, and Manuela Torres was his main hope now.

"You keep your promises," he said, smiling at her where she lay with her eyes closed beside him. She breathed deeply as if to hold the last hour inside her, to not return from where they had been together.

"And you are all you promise to be." She smiled up at him. "Do they all tell you that, Nick Carter? All the women you must make love to for their secrets?"

"Secrets are good," Carter said. "Lovemaking is better."

She laughed. "I wonder. For Lalita, I think, the secrets

are more exciting. Perhaps it is best I am a museum curator
and not some kind of player in your power games. All right,
what more do you want to ask me, American lover and
soldier of secrets?"

"What were you going to tell me about Lalita, Manuela?"

She lay in silence for a time in the dim afternoon room
behind the drawn shades, the myriad street noises of Madrid
outside. She seemed to listen to the city sounds.

"I am a lover of non-Western art and culture with too
many degrees who lives in a world with too few museums
where I can use my knowledge and abilities. When I was
approached by the Indian authorities to be curator of this
museum, it was an undreamed-of opportunity for a young
woman in my country, perhaps in most countries." Naked,
she turned on her side to look at Carter. "But from the
beginning I knew something was wrong. There was little or
no interest in attracting the public. Even the location is so
out of the way as to be ridiculous. It became very clear even
to someone as naïve as I was then that it was all a front for
something, and eventually I was told what."

She shook her head. "What could I do? What went on in
the rear half of my museum was not my concern. I knew
nothing of arms shipments and hostages and politics. I still
had a museum to operate, I was paid well, where else could
I go? So I stayed. Then something changed. Lalita appeared. She claimed to be an inspector for the Indian
government. Her job was to check the authenticity of our
exhibits, be sure they weren't stolen. She was sent to
catalogue all we had. It seemed legitimate at first, but then
there were too many times I found her where she was not
supposed to be."

"That's when you decided she was probably an agent of
the Indian secret service?"

"Yes."

"Did you tell the CIA people?"

"I am not a spy, Nick."

"No," he said. "Okay, now what about the terrorist attack a few weeks—?"

She put her hand over his mouth. "I haven't finished. You are as impatient a secret soldier as you are a lover."

"You prefer a patient lover the way Lalita does?"

Her eyes flashed in the dimness. "I prefer nothing about Lalita Chatterjee! The *Kama Sutra* is a great work of erotic literature. As a lovemaking manual I prefer something less refined, more physical, with sweat and passion."

They stared at each other, and Carter felt the surge in his groin. She wanted him again, he wanted her, but there was too much he needed to know.

"What else about Lalita?"

She took a deep, shuddering breath and turned her eyes away from him. Only her long, slim hand reached out to play with his rigidness. "Recently, in the last year or so, she has been different. It is hard to explain, but an anger has been growing in her. At first she was clearly a person doing her job. Now there is more. Now something is burning inside her, Nick. A personal commitment."

"To what?"

"I don't know that," she said, shaking her head. Then she turned to look at him again. "But I can tell you one aspect of her that is new, if it means anything or not. She has become much more interested in the art we have here. She stares at it now sometimes for hours, talks about it, asks me the history and meaning of each piece as if she is trying to learn about her own heritage."

The Killmaster remembered what Lalita had said to him in Dallas, that there could be a sudden resurgence of old-style pride in Hindu India. Cultural pride and nationalist pride. Maybe she'd been doing more than guessing. Maybe she'd been testing him for his reaction to the idea.

"Anything else, Manuela?"

"No."

"Then tell me all about the terrorist actions against you."

"There is nothing to tell. There were two bombs detonated outside the museum, some gunfire, written threats to the newspapers telling people to stay away from the opening of our new exhibit. We postponed the opening a week, then opened without fanfare and nothing has happened."

"No more threats?"

"None."

Carter frowned. "That's unusual. If they wanted to keep you from opening, you'd think they would have done more damage with their attack."

Manuela nodded, and watched the Killmaster. "It is almost as if they did not want to damage any of the art treasures, isn't it?"

"Yes," Carter said. "And that sounds almost like the Indian government itself. Unless—" He paused for a moment. "Was anything stolen? Anything missing?"

"A diversion? I thought of that, but nothing was taken."

"You're sure? Not a Sanskrit scroll about a thousand years old? Part of the *Bhagavad Gita,* I'd say. Something about the reluctant warrior Arjuna?"

In the hot afternoon room Manuela Torres sat up abruptly and stared down at Carter. "How could you know about that? Unless you're a CIA plant. Is that it, Nick? Is all this a test to find out if I will talk? Am I to be fired now?"

"Then you do know about that scroll?"

"Are you my enemy?"

"No, Manuela. I'm the enemy of terrorism in all its forms. Tell me about the scroll."

She sat there on the bed and went on staring at Carter, her naked body softened and muted by the dim light. She was like some slender northern doe with her pale skin and blond hair, her vulnerable wariness. "Perhaps," she said, staring at him where he lay on the bed, "Lalita Chatterjee was behind the attack. Perhaps she sent you here to frighten me or dazzle me or corrupt me. Get me to leave my job or close the museum." She watched Carter. "Perhaps you are working with her, have come to get close to me to destroy the secret part of the museum, but must destroy the good part with it so no one will know what you have really done and why."

Carter sat up and reached for her. He pulled her close to him. She resisted, then let go and shivered against him. "There is so much evil in this world, Nick. How can I be sure?"

"Trust your instincts. Trust what you feel about me, no matter what I do."

She slowly nodded. "All right. The scroll was here. It is more than a thousand years old, a magnificent treasure. But it was stolen months ago. It was taken by a greedy CIA agent who sold it for a fortune and vanished." Her pale blue eyes flashed with anger. "Sometimes I think these CIA people, always making their own deals, are more dangerous to us than the terrorists."

"Sometimes I think you're right," Carter admitted. "Do you know who bought the scroll from—"

Carter stopped in midsentence, swept Manuela Torres off the bed to the floor behind it, and pulled Wilhelmina from under his pillow all in a single motion.

He'd barely heard the soft footstep outside the apartment door, the faint click of the key in the lock.

He hit the floor, the 9mm Luger in hand, at the same instant as the bedroom door was flung open and a lethal fusillade of automatic fire raked and ripped the empty bed.

Silence.

For an endless second the small dark shape stood framed in the light of the open doorway, the Uzi in its hands.

Carter lay on the bedroom floor.

Manuela Torres huddled behind the bed. She screamed.

The dark figure fired another long, wild burst from the Uzi that hammered the walls and ceiling, smashed the shaded windows, raining shards of plaster and wallpaper and glass over the dim room. Then was gone.

Manuela Torres whimpered somewhere in fear.

Up, Carter was out through the living room into the long carpeted corridor of the expensive modern apartment building. Doors opened all along the hallway, and banged shut at the sight of the fleeing man with his Uzi, and the naked pursuer with a Luger. Terrorist attacks were an everyday fear in a nation so recently out from under a tyrannical fascism, where Basque separatists attacked often.

At the far end the small shape with the Uzi clawed open the door to the fire stairs and disappeared.

Carter raced after him.

Down the four flights of empty stairs the Killmaster heard the frantic running ahead of him. At the next to the last landing, a burst of Uzi fire raked the stairwell and Carter dived for cover.

But only for an instant.

On the steel and concrete the Killmaster rolled and came up already hurtling down the last flight of stairs to the door that had barely closed behind his quarry.

Across the lobby startled residents stared after the small figure in black with its Uzi as it vanished through the door into the street, and then at the naked man running in hot pursuit with a Luger in his hand.

Outside, Carter glimpsed the fleeing attacker turn the first corner into a narrower side street that led to the old city. The residents of the apartment building would be on the telephone by now calling, and it wouldn't be long before the Guardia Civil appeared to go after both Carter and his quarry.

He had to get the attacker before that, and could not risk being picked up now by the Spanish police.

At the corner he saw nothing.

The attacker had vanished.

But not from Nick Carter.

The Killmaster's trained eyes saw the faint movement in the shadow of a recessed doorway halfway up the silent and deserted side street.

Luger held down as if unaware of the danger, Carter crossed the narrow street and walked slowly along the opposite side to give the attacker in his doorway what would seem like a clear shot at the unsuspecting Carter.

He walked.

Saw the shifting, the movement in the shadow of the doorway.

Fell flat to the old sidewalk stones a split second before the Uzi raked the air where he had been a second before.

Wilhelmina out in both hands pointing straight at the shadowy recess, Carter called out, "Drop it! Now!"

It was then, in the suspended instant of standoff, Carter ready to roll away into another doorway if the Uzi fired again, that the attacker showed he was no professional. He neither fired again, nor surrendered. He ran.

He bolted out of the shadows and Carter saw him clearly for the first time: a short, dark man wearing narrow black cotton trousers, a long black tunic with a high collar, and a black Nehru hat. The Uzi was almost forgotten and dangled around his neck, steadied by one small brown hand as he fled.

The servile, and then not so servile, even arrogant, asistant to Manuela Torres at the Prince Alphonse Museum.

"Freeze!" Carter cried. He was up and braced spread-legged, Wilhelmina steady on the back of the fleeing hindu.

The man ran on in panic.

Carter fired two warning shots inches over the attacker's head. He wanted this one alive.

The panicked attacker stopped and stood frozen for a long minute with his back to Carter. He seemed to shudder, his shoulders suddenly shaking as if crying.

Then he turned.

The fear was like a twisted mask on his small, dark face.

But pride was there too.

Pride, and shame, and in the eyes a tortured fanaticism.

He raised the Uzi and cried out in Hindi, "Krishna is great!"

Carter went down the instant before the little submachine gun fired. The bullets whined over him, lowered toward the stones of the narrow street, and he had no choice.

The Killmaster fired twice.

Flung backward like a rag doll, the small man sprawled on his back on the stones, the Uzi firing one last burst into the sky as his finger tightened convulsively on the trigger.

Then there was only silence.

The distant sounds of the city and traffic.

Carter walked to the fallen man. He was dead. Both of
Carter's shots had hit an inch apart on the narrow chest.

Swearing, Carter quickly searched the still warm body.
The police would be here any second. He found nothing but
a small gold medallion around the neck of the assistant. He
grabbed it, pulled off the bloody tunic, and ran on around
the corner.

He put on the tunic and circled the long block of the
apartment. There was a side service entrance. Carter slipped
inside and worked his way to the rear stairs and up to
Manuela Torres's floor.

The corridor was deserted. No one had connected the
museum curator to the shooting. Carter slid silently along to
her door and knocked softly. It opened instantly, as if
Manuela had been waiting behind it ever since he'd left.
She probably had. Carter checked his watch: less than five
minutes had passed.

"Did you—?"

Carter nodded, then closed the door behind him. "He's
dead. Your assistant at the museum."

"Ranji? No!"

"Tell me about him. The Guardia will have found the
body by now, and they'll be heading for the museum to talk
to you."

"There's nothing to tell, Nick. His name is . . . was,
Ranji Mahrata. He came from the Delhi area, was well
educated and a first-rate assistant."

"He wasn't part of the CIA setup?"

"Not at all!"

"Did he know about it?"

"I'm not sure. If he did, he never said anything."

Carter showed her the medallion. It was solid gold,
looked new rather than old, and had carved figures on both
sides. Carter recognized the larger figure—Krishna himself,
tall in his chariot. The smaller figure on the other side was

unfamiliar—a warrior bare to the waist with a sword in each hand.

"It's Krishna," Manuela said, "and on the other side is the warrior of the *Bhagavad Gita,* Arjuna."

"Does it mean anything special? Or anything you know about?"

"No, except that it's a warrior's medal, and Ranji was in no way a warrior."

"He was at the end," Carter said grimly. "A dead warrior."

They stood silent for a time, Manuela still naked, Carter in the bloody tunic of the dead man. An echo of their so recent passion seemed to move through the room.

"What will you do now?" Manuela asked.

Carter smiled, wanly. "First, get dressed."

"Not quite yet. Please hold me . . ."

An hour later, Carter, dressed and ready to leave, asked her to send him her file on the dead Ranji Mahrata.

"Why not come and pick it up?"

"We'd better not be seen together. Send it to the airport by messenger for Nick Collins. I'll get it. Later, I'll bring it back personally."

"I'd like that," Manuela said. "Where will you go now?"

"To India."

He looked out into the corridor, kissed her, and slid out and down the stairs.

He hated to lie to a lady.

SIX

The telephone was in a secluded corner of the VIP lounge at Madrid's airport. Carter's United Nations ID got him into the lounge, and the coded number got him through to Hawk in his office in far-off Washington. AXE's director was not in a good mood.

"You took your time, Nick. I hope the results were worth it."

Carter reported all that had happened—with the exception of his afternoon with Manuela Torres.

"There seem to be a few hours missing somewhere," Hawk mused wryly from his penthouse office. Carter grinned as he heard the lighter flick, the puffing to get the cigar started. "Then it's your opinion that both the Star of India in Dallas, and the Prince Alphonse Museum are essentially fronts for our CIA chums in their business affairs with Pakistan, the Afghans, and most other points east?"

"Correct," Carter said.

"Where do Chatterjee and Torres fit into the picture?"

"I'd say Lalita was an Indian secret service agent, but according to Manuela she's been acting odd lately."

55

"Odd? How?"

"A surge of superpatriotism, the glory of the past, Mother India rampant."

"And Torres?"

"She's just what she seems. An educated woman with few places to use her knowledge and skill who had to take an offer even if she knew it was a front. There's a museum, she's its curator. The worst she's done is shut her eyes to the Company's hanky-panky, keep her mouth shut."

"Perhaps," Hawk said across the distance, puffing harder on the cigar. "The bombings? The shootings? The attack on you?"

"I don't know about the shooting in Los Angeles yet. It doesn't seem to fit," Carter said. "But the two bombings have to be the work of some group opposed to the CIA-Pakistan connection and all the hardware and havoc they ship into South Asia."

"The man who tried to kill you and Manuela Torres?"

"An educated, proud Hindu who wore a gold medallion to Krishna the Charioteer and the solider Arjuna. He was playing the humble act as Manuela Torres's assistant. My guess is he was really there to spy on the CIA-Pakistan operation."

The sound of puffing conjured up a picture of clouds of smoke in a dim room. "Sum it up, Nick."

"There's a new group somewhere in India dedicated to the rebirth of Hindu power, the destruction of Pakistan, of CIA influence, probably of modern Western ways in everything. A kind of fundamentalist Hindu movement. They have Krishna as their symbol, Arjuna and the *Bhagavad Gita* as their inspiration. What else, or who and where and how, I don't know yet."

"But you will," the distant chief of AXE said. "Yes, that's about how we read it here. A cultural resurgence that turned bad. Maybe on its own, maybe with some help."

"I go to India?"

"You have any leads to where to go?"

"Only Ranji Mahrata."

There was a long silence. Not even the cigar puffing. "Not enough, Nick. We need more. I can get working here, but it might not be fast enough. We don't know enough about whoever these people are to know what to be afraid of."

"Maybe the death of Ranji Mahrata will smoke someone out, bring them here. I'll stake out the museum for a few days."

"That could be damned dangerous."

"It could also pay off."

The silence was shorter. "All right, but keep in close touch. With any luck we'll come up with a lead first."

After he hung up, Carter waited in the lounge until the hollow voice of the airport announcer asked for Señor Nick Collins to come to the airport manager's office. It was the file on Ranji Mahrata from Manuela Torres. Carter identified himself with yet another phony ID, signed for the package, and left.

It was time to find a hotel, rent a car, and start watching the Prince Alphonse Museum. With any luck, everyone would think he was already in India.

A slow dawn over the Castilian metropolis found Carter in a rented Citroën parked up the narrow street from the Prince Alphonse Museum.

He watched Manuela Torres arrive dressed in black, and then a cortege of solemn Indians obviously coming to ask questions and pay their respects to the boss of the late Ranji Mahrata. At noon, Manuela left in a black chauffeur-driven limousine for what was probably a memorial service. The dead Indian assistant would almost certainly be sent home for a proper Hindu funeral pyre.

It was then that Carter noticed the other car staked out and watching the museum.

A nondescript gray Ford, it had been parked only a few cars away from Carter. Now it pulled out to follow Manuela Torres in her limousine. Carter had a clear view of two men in dark suits and ties. Young, clean-cut types. Hatless, one blond and the other sandy-haired. They had Langley, Virginia, written all over them. Which was logical. The death of the assistant would have alarmed them, since they wouldn't have any idea who had done it or why, and they would have become very suspicious that poor Ranji Mahrata had been more than he seemed. The Company didn't like the idea that someone who had been close to them hadn't been sufficiently checked out.

Carter did not follow Manuela or the CIA men.

He waited.

The third car appeared an hour later.

It was a battered green Volkswagen van that drove slowly along the street in front of the museum. Too slowly. It almost stopped twice, as if to study entrances and exits, then disappeared around the far corner.

Only to reappear again half an hour later and go through the same slow drive-by routine.

This time the van windows were too small and dirty for Carter to see the occupants, but he had a pretty good hunch they would be Hindu Indians, probably wearing the same Krishna the Charioteer and Arjuna medallion that the late Ranji Mahrata had worn.

They did not appear a third time.

The limousine returned with Manuela Torres and an elegant, grim-looking, dark-skinned gentleman in formal civilian attire but the telltale ramrod manner of a general and an important general. In this case the analysis of the dark man's manner wasn't even necessary. Carter recognized Major General Nazir al-Ahmad, the emerging new power of the assassinated Zia ul-Haq's party in Pakistan. The good general would be there to find out what a Hindu art scholar could possibly have been doing in a CIA front to get himself killed.

General Nazir would be more than a little annoyed when the CIA and Manuela Torres couldn't tell him. In a different location, in his own not-too-happy country, he would have ways to make Manuela tell what she and Carter had guessed

about Ranji Mahrata, but the CIA wouldn't want trouble
with a Spanish national in her own country.

Carter hoped they wouldn't anyway, and was relieved to
see General Nazir stalk out of the museum an hour later in
obvious anger. One of the clean-cut Langley men who'd
been in the gray Ford walked a step behind him explaining
something the general did not want to hear. Keeping
international princelings happy so they could be bulwarks
against communism wasn't an easy job for young men used
to getting everything they asked for from an eager president
and a compliant Congress.

Nothing more happened until the museum closed and
Manuela Torres left looking lovely and more than a little
sad. Carter sighed, but he couldn't let her know he was still
in Madrid and watching her. There was no certainty which
side she was on.

By midnight he gave up and went back to his hotel for a
few hours of sleep.

With the sun next morning, Carter was back, in a white
Mercedes this time, parked at the opposite end of the
museum.

The gray Ford was in the same spot a block away. Too
much easy power breeds arrogance, and arrogance breeds
carelessness and a neglect of fundamentals. The Company
men were asking to be spotted. Young and not too bright.

The man who appeared only minutes after dawn was not
too young and a lot more than bright. Yassar Arawan, the
dissident PLO leader, vanished inside the museum as if he'd
been expected. Less than twenty minutes later, the notori-
ous Muslim terrorist and anti-Shi'ite fanatic, Hamid
Hameesh, arrived on a motorcycle and vanished around the
building to where Carter knew there was a side door into the
off-limits storehouse portion of the building.

If the Killmaster had had any doubts about what the Prince
Alphonse really was, they were gone now. All the CIA-
backed, anti-Soviet, anti-Chinese, anti-Khomeini troops were
gathering to try to figure out what the unexplained violent

death of a simple scholar meant for their cause and safety.
There was no surprise in it for Carter.

And no surprise for someone else.

The battered green Volkswagen van appeared again at the
museum just before noon.

Again it cruised slowly along the street.

But this time two more almost identical vans, one brown
and one yellow, followed it. Carter sat up, alert. He looked
along the block toward the gray Ford. The two young CIA
men hadn't seemed to notice the parade of old vans that
disappeared once more around the first corner.

Carter checked his weapons and waited. He didn't want
to move too soon, but if what he suspected was going down,
he would have to take some action.

It could be the break he needed, but timing would be
vital.

He waited.

The green van came around once more.

It parked in a loading zone across the street from the
museum and sat there. The other two vans did not return.

The two CIA men still did nothing.

Carter got out of the Mercedes and walked quickly across
the street to the front entrance of the museum. It was a risk.
The guys in the van might be spooked and he'd lose them.
The CIA could recognize him, or at least be startled by a
stranger hurrying into the museum. But he owed Manuela
Torres at least a chance.

He went in and strode through the magnificent exhibits of
a thousand years of Indian art and culture to Manuela's
office at the rear. She looked up and stared as he came in.

"Nick? I thought—"

"Grab the most valuable treasure you have. Get your
people out with everything they can carry. Hurry!"

The slim blond curator stood. "I don't understand.
Why—?"

"No time, dammit! Just hurry!"

Manuela picked up the interoffice phone, pressed one

button after the other, and spoke rapidly. She put the receiver down.

"What is—?"

"Grab something yourself, and come on!"

She stood frozen. "Tell me what is going on, Nick."

The American voice spoke behind Carter. "Yeah, mister, tell us what's going on too."

The two CIA men from the gray Ford stood behind him in the office with their pistols leveled. This kind of action they understood.

"Who the hell are you?" the second demanded.

"Talk fast," the first ordered.

"Nick, please—" Manuela said.

"Nick?" the first CIA man repeated.

Out in the museum Carter could hear Manuela's people moving, hurrying toward the doors. It was too late for those in the office to get out in time now. He calmly sat down in one of Manuela's Barcelona chairs.

"All right," he said. "There are three vans outside. Two of them are loaded with explosives and are probably parked against the walls of this building now. The third is out front in a loading zone right near where you two clowns were staked out in your Ford. It will have the detonator in it. They're going to destroy this building. I don't know when they planned to set it off, probably during lunch hour to spare as many of the museum staff as possible. But now they'll move when they see the first person leave carrying an object."

"Jesus, Sam, it must be the AV!" the second CIA man cried. "We'd better get the fuck—"

"Nick," the first said slowly, staring at Carter. "You're Carter, N3 of AXE. Why didn't—"

"I think," Carter said, "we'd all better get down, get under what we can, and hope the bomb isn't near this office."

He stood, grabbed Manuela, and pulled her down under her desk. She resisted until she had the statue of the dancing Shiva, then lay under the desk on top of it.

"It's the best of its kind in existence," she explained.

The two young CIA men just stared at them.

"What's the AV?" Carter asked.

"Arms of Vengeance," the first said.

"We've got to take those bastards out," the second said.

"Shut up," the first said, and faced Carter. "If you really think there's a bomb, we'd better try to find—"

The explosion flung the CIA men across the office and shook the earth itself under where Carter lay half covering Manuela Torres who covered the dancing Shiva. Plaster, wood, and glass rained down onto the desktop over their heads.

The second explosion blew in the whole outside wall just beyond the office and brought beams crashing down all through the massive building. They could hear wails of terror, and the awful sounds of smashing and tearing and collapsing. Dust and dirt and shards filled the suddenly hot air.

Then silence.

The screams and groans began.

Carter was up. The office was like an island in a sea of destruction. Manuela Torres stood up, her face a mask of shock. She looked around her. The partition walls had collapsed revealing the interior of the whole massive building. She clutched the superb thousand-year-old terra-cotta Shiva. "Why? Why? Why do people do this, Nick? Why?"

"To get what they want for themselves," Carter said grimly. He ran to the CIA men. They were both dead under the collapsed walls and beams. He turned to Manuela. "I'll be back someday."

Then he was out through the rubble and choking dust and gaping holes in the front wall to where the green Volkswagen van was pulling away from the loading zone across the narrow street. He leaped into his Mercedes and roared off after the van. It turned the first corner on two wheels, Carter close behind.

The rear door of the van burst open and assault rifles fired at the Killmaster. He swerved back and forth to escape the hail of bullets, clinging grimly to the van as it drove deeper into the narrow streets and alleys of the old city.

Wilhelmina in his left hand, Carter drove with his right and fired at the van's tires.

The terrorist vehicle swerved wildly to escape his fire.

A figure fell screaming out of the rear door.

Carter hit the man, ran over him, and drove on.

The van turned a narrow corner.

Carter was close behind and saw the man leap from the slowed van. Before the Killmaster could evade, the dark, fierce-eyed terrorist shot his tires out with an Uzi. The Mercedes smashed into the wall, the impact tearing open the door and sending Wilhelmina flying. The agile attacker laughed, then leaped to finish off Carter.

Hugo jumped out of Carter's sleeve into his hand, and was hurled in a single motion into the throat of the triumphant attacker. Surprise, hate, anger, and horror all filled the man's eyes as he fell dead in his own blood that spurted from his throat.

Carter whirled.

The van was gone.

"Damn!"

He swiftly bent to the dead man. Around his brown neck was another medallion of Krishna the Charioteer and the warrior Arjuna.

Windows were opening and people were shouting. Carter picked up Wilhelmina, abandoned the wrecked Mercedes, and ran back the way he had come. The man he had hit and run over lay on his back. Some Madrileños were there trying to help him. When they saw Carter, they scattered. The man was dead, staring up from shocked eyes. The same medallion was around his throat.

Carter turned off into the side streets and ran on.

He sat again in the secluded corner of the VIP lounge at the Madrid airport. The bombing, and the mysterious killings of two of the terrorists, was all over the headlines.

But Carter's ID and disguise were proof against any possibility of discovery. AXE did its work well.

"The Arms of Vengeance?" David Hawk said. "That fits, Nick. Now we know what we're looking for."

"I'm booked for Calcutta in an hour."

"That won't be too soon," Hawk said grimly. "See what you can do by tracing Ranji Mahrata's recent associations and actions, but my guess is they'll have covered any trail by now."

"At least we know what we're looking for," Carter said. "A fundamentalist Hindu group named the Arms of Vengeance that follows Krishna and the *Bhagavad Gita*."

"Now all we have to do is learn what they plan to do, what their goals are, and stop them." Hawk was chewing on the stump of his foul cigar now. "We have a man, Philip Shelby, in Calcutta. He's CIA, but he, ah, sometimes works with us. The Company is not always to his liking."

"I can try to infiltrate, try to get some of the AV people to come over to us."

Hawk's chewing went on across the distance. "I doubt you'll get very far that way, Nick. The U.S. has made too many commitments to Pakistan and other Muslim nations for the Hindus to trust us."

"Then I'll have to neutralize them," Carter said quietly.

"First, however, you'll have to find them."

SEVEN

Calcutta

Nick Carter moved slowly along the crowded, stinking streets of the massive city on the edge of the Bay of Bengal. Dressed as a one-eyed begger, the Killmaster limped with seeming obliviousness through the hordes of near naked, half-starved natives whose only home was the streets. In the city of over ten million people, the streets and the mammoth railroad station were not only their home but their history.

Here, against a wall on the open sidewalk, they were born, lived, loved, and died. In a world where some had so much, these had nothing. Poverty, overpopulation, starvation, unemployment. The problems of India—and of the world. Horrors that went on and on while nations spent billions on weapons and violence and wars that would probably never happen, and fanatics put all their energy into hollow dreams of ethnicism and nationalism and the empty pride of being the rulers of somewhere no matter how small and poor.

Nowhere was the stupidity and inhumanity of man more obvious than in Calcutta with its crush of human misery against the imposing stone buildings of a dead British Empire. If the British had thought of human needs instead of buildings, of the Indians instead of themselves, of humanity instead of empire, they might have left a real legacy instead of the shame that is Calcutta.

Carter thought all this as, disguised as one of them, he pushed and jostled through the hordes who walked, bathed, cooked, and slept on the sidewalks. Until he reached a brass shop in a small street off Dalhousie Square. There, he limped inside to the consternation of the shopkeeper who hurried forward, abandoning a customer, to shoo him out in rapid Bengali.

"Go! Go! You have no right to be in my shop!"

Carter bobbed and weaved as he evaded the man's attempts to push him out, but it was the customer his gaze rested on. A six-foot-six giant who must have weighed in at 250 pounds, this man wore a broad-brimmed gray felt hat, a belted bush jacket and chino trousers, and brandished an ebony cane with a silver head shaped in the form of a unicorn. His left foot was in a heavy walking cast, but he now clumped nimbly forward to the shopkeeper. He too spoke in Bengali.

"Why don't you just give the chap a rupee or two and be done with it, my man?"

The shopkeeper bridled, then spoke against his own interest in selling the customer. "This is not your concern, Englishman. Out, you rabble, out!"

Carter drew himself up and spoke in street Bengali the same as the other two. "I am also a citizen of great Calcutta. I have a right to enter any shop. You are lucky I do not have my ax with me, shopkeeper."

"Ax? What is this jabbering of axes? Go, you filth!"

The giant Englishman stared at Carter. Carter winked, then seemed to collapse and turn away to limp from the shop.

Outside he limped on along the teeming sidewalk away

from the great square toward the waterfront. The old
Bentley drew up beside him as he reached the harbor. The
passenger door opened. Carter glanced around, and slipped
inside. The giant from the brass shop drove off quickly and
said nothing until they were out of the downtown area and
on their way to the suburb of Howrah.

"Carter?"

"Right," the Killmaster said. "Hawk's told you what
we're after?"

"The Arms of Vengeance," Philip Shelby said. "A tall
order, and there isn't too much time if my assessment of the
danger is anywhere near correct."

"Is that what you've told the Company?"

Carter studied the giant. A noted Sanskrit scholar who
had remained and become an Indian citizen after the British
left, his lifelong project was a definitive biography of the
great Bengali poet Girsha Ghosh. This made him a darling
of the governments of West Bengal and India, and of the
upper-class Hindu gentry. It gave him almost unlimited
access to the really powerful of Hindu India. In fact, as
Carter knew from Hawk, Shelby was a cultural anthropol-
ogist who reported sometimes to the CIA, was reputed to
still be close to British intelligence, and—sometimes known
only to Hawk—worked whenever he was asked for AXE.

Shelby laughed. "My generous friends back in Langley
have little interest in what they see as, and I quote, 'a bunch
of nuts in diapers bowing down to statues with six arms and
big tits.' When you work for the Company, you learn to
give them essentially what they ask for and very little more.
They do not encourage imagination in their local snoops.
That's why I find it much more interesting to work with
your David Hawk." The big man grinned at Carter. "Especially if it means in some way screwing my CIA buddies,
right?"

Carter watched the big man. There was something about
Shelby that disturbed him. An arrogance, a disdain, that put
himself above his work. When an agent came to believe he
was smarter than the service he worked for, it could be

deadly. It all becomes a game, a charade, in which life and death are just points in a contest. No right and wrong, only the play.

"How'd you get into intelligence work anyway?" Carter asked casually, removing some of his disguise as they drove. "It's a far cry from cultural anthropology or Bengali poets."

"The service first, of course. Cold war and all that. MI5 tried to recruit me while I was at University, but I wasn't interested at the time. After I went into the army out here, they came around and made me an offer I couldn't refuse. Later, when Nehru was leading us to a secure independence, he asked me to help train an Indian intelligence service, work for it as long as I wanted. It was a zoo out here right after independence, every little foreign agent trying to subvert us, and I did my bit." He laughed again. "MI5 never did realize I was doubling for Nehru. They kept wondering why so many of their schemes to hang on here went awry. But Nehru died, and I had little loyalty to the new mob. That's when Langley approached me and I thought it would be interesting to keep my hand in."

"And AXE?"

"Ah, that's a different matter. Your David Hawk is a man who believes in what he does, and does what he believes in. Let's say we're both working for a truly better world."

It was all smooth and glib, but Carter still had the sense that everything was a game, a contest, to Shelby. With a man like that you never knew what was true and what was a smoke screen. What was honest, and what was part of the game. He could be a loyal CIA man fooling Hawk, or still in Indian intelligence fooling both the CIA and Hawk, or perhaps had never left MI5 at all and was fooling everyone. Or he could be exactly what he said he was, a trained intelligence agent now out to follow his own principles and who had found AXE to be an organization he could work for.

"Tell me about the Arms of Vengeance," Carter said. "How did you learn about them?"

Shelby nodded, but said nothing. The big man's eyes were fixed on the rearview mirror of the Bentley. "I think we have a curious friend."

Carter looked back.

"The second car," Shelby said. "Black Citroën. It's been with us since the waterfront."

"You or me?"

"Hard to say. Could be either. The more important question is, who is it? I've known the police to drive unmarked Citroëns. Indian intelligence could be anywhere."

"But you don't think so."

"No." Shelby watched the distant black car. It was the only car behind them now, and came on steadily, neither gaining nor falling back. "My guess would be the AV, or the CIA/Pakistani crew. They could have picked you up in Madrid and tailed you all the way."

"No," Carter said. "No one could have tailed me after I went underground to meet you."

Shelby glanced at him coolly. "You're so sure?"

"I'm sure."

Shelby looked back at the road ahead as they were entering the neat suburbs with the Howarth railroad station off to the left. "Then it has to be the chaps watching me."

"You think someone is watching you?"

"I know so," Shelby said. "How do you think I got this present on my foot?"

"Tell me."

The big agent shrugged. "Little to tell, except it was no bloody accident. Four thugs I couldn't identify cornered me a block from my house out here. I was on my evening walk, and fought the bastards off, but their car ran over my foot in the melee and they got away."

"No idea who they were?"

"Indians, but nothing more."

"Why?"

Shelby made quick turns through the suburban streets, his eyes watching the rearview mirror. After the third sharp turn and some doubling back, he smiled.

"Lost them." He drove faster. "Why? Because I have been making my own private investigation of the Arms of Vengeance for the last six months. There can't be any other reason."

Carter studied the big man's profile. "Alone?"

"Yes." His massive hands whitened on the steering wheel of the old Bentley. "This is my country, Carter. I love it and its people, want to see it forge ahead into a secure future. That is why I work for anyone I think will help India and oppose anyone I think will harm her."

Grim-faced now, Shelby continued to drive slowly through the quieter streets of the suburbs, turning and twisting to confuse any possible pursuit. "A year or so ago I stumbled across the Arms of Vengeance. It appeared to be no more than another small organization of upper-caste Hindus devoted to a cultural revival of the great past. But there were small things that disturbed me."

"Such as?"

"A strong emphasis on the militant aspects of the heritage, and a certain secrecy. A fanaticism that didn't sound like that of an organization devoted to the glories of art and culture. For example, most such groups have always emphasized the importance of the Brahman and Ksatriyana castes, the sages and scholars. But AV appears dedicated to *kshatrya*, the warrior ethos. Militant and secret."

"So you went after them?"

"As far as I could. I managed to infiltrate the fringes through my contacts and helped them raise funds. But I'm not a true Indian, not a born Hindu, have no caste at all, so I am only an outsider who is tolerated but not trusted to be allowed in. My hope is that you can do better."

"Why? I'm not Hindu. Not even Indian."

"No, but you represent real power, real money. Lately I've sensed they need and want money, and where better to get it than from the generous United States?"

"What do they need money for?"

"According to them, to buy back art treasures, to set up centers of culture throughout the nation to make the people more aware of the glories of the Hindu past long before the Moghuls came down. To establish camps to teach boys the past."

"But?"

Shelby slowed and turned into the driveway of a long, low half-Western-, half-Indian-style house with enormous trees that spread low branches over the entire house. An open courtyard stood in the center around a shimmering reflecting pool, with the house around it on three sides. Inside, the shadows of servants moved behind the bamboo shades. He parked, but did not get out.

"But I think they have more than culture in mind. I think we're dealing with a kind of Irish Republican Army situation here, Carter. There is a public wing of the Arms of Vengeance that raises money and buys art and establishes cultural centers with the help and blessing of many of our most respected high-caste citizens. Then there is another wing."

"Secret and militant like the provisional wing of the IRA? The Provos and Sinn Fein?"

"Exactly. I haven't been able to pick up much, but there have been hints, whispers—mostly from my Muslim contacts—of the buying of weapons, the training of a cadre of militant warriors, and, recently, attacks on those they consider their enemies outside India."

"How are they fronting the arms buying?"

"Mostly with traveling art exhibits, and through Hindu scholars abroad who have joined them, or have been frightened into helping with threats. Remember the museum curator in Los Angeles, Ramdass Ghosh, who was shot down right in his museum? My whisperers say he was actually a member of AV, and was buying weapons from the illegal arms people in Southern California and Mexico."

"Do your whisperers say who got him?"

Shelby nodded. "A Pakistani agent I know only too well. Her name is Nasrim Nasrullah Khan. Her great-grandfather was a hard-nosed border prince it took the British forty years to subdue, and her grandfather and father both fought to get the British and the Hindus out of their territory. Nasrim's as tough or tougher. They say she has the Sword of God tattooed on her breasts so she can see it every time she goes to bed."

"Nice lady," Carter muttered.

Shelby laughed. "As a matter of fact she's damn nice, both in and out of bed. Just never cross her."

The big man got out of the Bentley, waited for Carter, then went up the shaded path among the lush vegetation. He leaned heavily on his cane, dragging the foot with the walking cast. Carter followed him toward the covered veranda that ran around the entire building. As they mounted the two steps to the door, Carter stopped.

"Shelby!"

The big agent froze, stood motionless.

"What?"

Carter stared at the double front door.

A tiny wire was almost invisible just under the gleaming brass handle.

"You have an alarm system?"

"No."

A brass bell hung beside the door with a long colorful silk cord for pulling the clapper to announce a visitor. There was no doorbell.

"Then—"

The door swung open!

"Ah, master—!"

Carter slammed into the big man, sending them both sprawling into the tropical shrubbery as the explosion rocked the whole house.

Glass shattered. Wood ripped. The stink of the plastic explosive washed over them through the thick humid air.

And over it all the sickening echo of a long, strangled scream.

The torn and bloody body of the smiling servant lay quivering on the destroyed veranda.

EIGHT

Voices rose throughout the neighborhood, doors slammed, feet came running. In the shattered house the other servants stood staring through the debris at their mangled coworker. Shelby struggled to stand on his broken foot and leaned heavily on his cane as he stared at the wreckage of his house.

"I owe you one," he said.

"The police'll be here any minute," Carter said. "They know you. They don't know me. They'll ask questions. I don't have time."

Shelby handed Carter his car keys. "Drive to this address." It was handwritten on a business card. Shelby worked prepared for emergencies. "Hold up, and I'll be there as soon as I get rid of the cops and see if I can find any evidence of who set the booby trap for me."

"Or me," Carter added.

"Unlikely. They would have had no way of knowing where I would take you, probably figured anywhere except my own house. Anyway, go. I'll be there as soon as I can."

Carter nodded, ran to the Bentley, and drove out through

the throng of chattering neighbors now gathered in front of
Shelby's bombed house. There was more than curiosity in
the eyes and voices. There was fear. Violence was part of
life in India, but not in this elite neighborhood. Not until
now.

He turned the first corner, and then slowed to a lazy
speed. A police car rushing past to the scene didn't even
slow as it passed. Carter was a European in a Bentley, a fine
old one in a good area. He couldn't possibly be a bomber.
Old habits, training, and prejudices die hard. They had
served the British Raj so long, it was all but impossible for
the average Indian to not defer to, bow to, the European.

Carter pulled the map of the city out of the glove
compartment and located the address Shelby had given him.
It was no more than a mile away, farther out in the
countryside. The Killmaster speeded up.

He watched the rearview mirror.

No one was following him.

The long Indian twilight lay on the thick gardens outside
the isolated country house where Nick Carter stood at the
window watching. Shelby was taking a long time. Carter
held Wilhelmina. He'd been watching and waiting for an
hour.

Was Shelby setting him up?

The booby trap had been a sloppy job, the wire exposed
for Carter to see. Amateurs, or a clever play to lull him into
trusting Shelby?

But the Killmaster trusted nobody.

He checked Pierre—his miniature gas bomb taped tight to
his inner thigh. Hugo was secure in its chamois sheath up
his sleeve. In the house he had found two AK-47s, fully
loaded and with extra ammunition. He was ready.

The twilight faded into the black Indian night. A jackal
cried somewhere.

A car sounded in the distance, came closer, and stopped.

Carter switched off the single light and waited at the
window.

Nothing happened for some time.

A twig snapped.

The giant figure seemed to appear out of nowhere not twenty feet from the dark and silent house.

Philip Shelby leaned on his cane, an Ingram submachine gun looking no bigger than a pistol in his other hand. Carter was impressed. Even with his foot in cast, the big agent moved with the skill and silence of a panther. Maybe Shelby would be good to work with after all.

Silent and cautious, Shelby stood in the shadows and studied the dark house without making a move to call out or enter until he was sure there was no trap. Even his own Bentley parked under a giant banyan tree did not make him assume Carter was there alone, or even there at all. It made Carter feel that faint hint of doubt again—how had Shelby missed the booby-trap wire at his house that Carter had seen so quickly? A moment of carelessness on stepping into familiar territory? Or something else?

Carter also waited.

There was no certainty Shelby was alone.

Both men listened, probed with their senses like human radar stations.

It was Shelby who spoke first.

"Carter? You're here. I'm coming in."

The Killmaster watched the big agent clump slowly across the heavy duff under the trees and tangle of vines and thick growth, and step onto the covered veranda of the house. Shelby tried the front door and found it unlocked. A locked door couldn't stop any attack, and made escape that much harder.

Shelby smiled, then pushed the door all the way open. He came inside with his Ingram lowered. He closed the door.

Carter switched on the single lamp.

"What took so long?"

"Our Indian friends are not as easily put off as they used to be. They took me to the inspector, and we had a nice long chat. I told him, of course, that I had no idea who would want me dead, but that perhaps it was an enemy from my

intelligence past. I didn't fool him, but there wasn't much
he could do. He knows the government will vouch for me.
Past services to the nation and all that."

"I didn't come into it?"

"Not a whisper. Any alarms here?"

"Not a sound."

"Good. Ready to go?"

"Go where?"

"To an elegant party," Shelby said. "An exotic fund-
raiser for our friends the Arms of Vengeance. Very posh,
very exclusive. By personal invitation only."

"How do I get in?"

"Through the front door with me," Shelby said with a
grin. "They are more than eager to meet Mr. Nicholas
Craig, a very rich, very conservative American oil tycoon."

"Let's go."

Shelby laughed. "First you clean off that Calcutta dirt,
and put on the monkey suit I have in the car. The British are
gone, but they left their snobbery behind. It's strictly black
tie and tiaras."

The house of "Rip" Ramprasad was a vast, imposing
mansion straight out of the British Raj in the most exclusive
section of Calcutta where not that many years ago no Indian
could set foot except through the servants' entrance. The
section was now occupied by the rich commercial Brits who
still owned much of the country, the sons and daughters of
nizams and maharajahs, and the new Hindu elite who really
ran the nation.

A European butler took Shelby's and Carter's invitations,
then directed them to the study where the master waited to
greet the men while his lush wife in a gold sari welcomed
the ladies in the main room that was furnished entirely in
ancient regal Hindu tradition. Carter could see that many of
the women resented this pointed return to the past, as did
some of the men.

"Our host," Shelby said as they entered the smoke-filled
study where fifty men in dinner jackets smoked and drank,

"is determined to turn back not only the clock but the calendar."

Rip Ramprasad turned out to be a small, brisk, forty-year-old who stood out among the dinner jackets in a traditional long silver tunic, narrow black trousers, soft shoes trimmed with silver, and a turban interwoven with silver and gold threads. He seemed totally confident with his oversize Havana cigar and discreet snifter of the best brandy. Obviously the truly elite guests had already had dinner in some secluded dining room of the vast mansion, the more ordinary invited only for the after-dinner activities.

"Ramprasad," Shelby explained in a low voice as they waited for their host to get around to welcoming them, "is the scion of an ancient, once powerful Brahman family forced for centuries into a backseat position under the Muslim rulers. The Moghuls ruled them, but never took their wealth, and after the British came they emerged to become even richer in commercial enterprises. British prejudice never extended to not doing business with natives who had a great deal of money and influence. In fact, such families were actively adopted, thoroughly Europeanized, their sons and daughters sent to England to become more British than the British. Rip, for example, acquired an Oxford degree as his father had, the preppy nickname, and a fine British accent with little Hindi intonation. He then went on to study business at Harvard and on Wall Street, and has about tripled the already obscenely large family fortune."

"Now he wants to turn back the centuries with it?" Carter said. "End his and India's Europeanization?"

"It would seem so," Shelby said softly as their host arrived to smile and extend a soft, languid brown hand.

"Ah, Shelby. Always a pleasure, the nation owes you much, eh?" He turned to study Carter. "This will be Mr. Craig?"

"Mr. Nicholas Craig of Dallas, Texas, yes," Shelby introduced.

Rip Ramprasad smiled with his thin mouth but not his eyes as he studied Carter, almost X-raying him. "And you are interested in the glories of our ancient Hindu culture, Mr. Craig?"

"Ever since I saw a traveling exhibition in Fort Worth many years ago, Mr. Ramprasad," Carter said. "Speaking of exhibitions, isn't it terrible what happened to the curator of that show currently on exhibit in Los Angeles?"

"Ah, you know about poor Ramdass? Yes, a tragedy, but that is the way of our violent enemies, Mr. Craig. The sword is all the unclean know."

"That puzzles me a little," Carter said. "I mean, why would you name a cultural revival the Arms of Vengeance? Sounds more than a little violent to me."

Rip Ramprasad smiled. "Then you have come to the right place to hear your answer. In a few moments I shall be calling the gathering to order for a short welcoming speech by myself before we start the business of taking pledges. Now, if you will excuse me, I must prepare. Make yourself at home, Mr. Craig. This house holds many fine art treasures of our culture for you to examine."

With a nod to Shelby, the small, slim man left, his Indian dress making him stand out like someone with a spotlight on him as he walked through the throng of dinner-jacketed men and into another room.

"Smooth," Carter said.

"Very," Shelby agreed. "And perhaps dangerous."

The European butler appeared to strike a resonant gong and announce that everyone was to gather in the main room for an address of welcome by Mr. Ramprasad, after which there would be entertainment and the taking of pledges. Carter and Shelby moved along the corridor and into the large main room with the rest. For the most part the people were all Indians, Carter and Shelby standing out. There was an eagerness, almost a euphoria to the crowd that left the two agents even more isolated.

In the large room that had once been a formal European living room, all traces of the West were gone. Statues and carved reliefs of the Indian pantheon stood everywhere, hung on the walls, and the center of the room was a large open space of bare, polished wood. Incense burned, and cushions and long futon-style mats were scattered tastefully on raised platforms around the open floor. The women in saris lounged comfortably, but those in Western evening dresses seemed awkward on the cushions, and most of the men stood in their dinner jackets.

Almost at once, Rip Ramprasad appeared, strode to the highest platform, and sat in a lotus position on a great gold cushion. He smiled, bowed to all four corners of the vast room, and began to speak.

"We are all worshippers of Krishna the Charioteer, devotees of the glory of our ancient culture, or we would not be here. Even those few here who are not of our culture are drawn to it like a moth to a great flame. Let me, then, be brief. We are here to honor, support, and cherish the Arms of Vengeance, an organization that has already done much to return us to the bosom of our ancestors, and will soon do much more."

His dark eyes seemed to burn as he stared at the silent assemblage. "It is time for us to become again what we once were! To lead this subcontinent and the world. For this I am convinced that the only way is a return to the old ways, the old tradition. To long before not only the Europeans, but before the Muslim invaders stole from us our country and our culture. It is time to once more call on the warrior Arjuna! To gird our loins and enlist behind our great warrior caste of *kshatrya*. Beginning today we are no longer Brahmans or any other of our great castes, we are all *kshatrya*, the warriors for the culture of Krishna the Charioteer, of Shiva, and of Kali! We are all warriors for the true Mother India. We are the Arms of Vengeance! All *kshatrya, kshatrya, kshatrya!*"

Even the women were on their feet now. They shouted as if they were one voice.

"Kshatrya! Kshatrya!"

Fists in the air, the men all shouted and began to chant the

Sanskrit word like an hypnotic war cry. The women screamed as if in a trance of rage.

Only then did Carter look around and see the young men, bare to the waist in flowing Hindu trousers with ancient golden Hindu helmets, who had appeared all around the room, swords menacing in their hands.

NINE

"Kshatrya!"

The echo of the shouting voices rang through the room and was taken up at the end by the sword-wielding young men all around the walls.

Both Shelby and Carter had their hands on their weapons, when Shelby suddenly whispered, "Christ, they're just kids."

"Not all," Carter said quietly.

The Killmaster nodded to one young man at each wall who seemed to be the leader. But the rest were all no more than eleven or twelve. Babies playing ancient soldier.

For a long minute after the last echo of the shouts had died away, Rip Ramprasad sat staring with burning eyes as if he could see Krishna himself exhorting the warrior Arjuna to battle. Then his face relaxed, and he smiled at the boys standing proudly with their swords.

"These are what the Arms of Vengeance is about. In camps and classes and weekly meetings throughout the country we will teach these future warriors for India about their past. A past that has been lost in the tide of modern-

81

ism, commercialism, welfarism. Our heritage has been
taken from these boys; we will give it back. Our country has
been taken from us; we will take it back with knowledge of
our past. From the past comes the future. From the present
as it is, comes only spiritual death. We will take back our
culture and our country."

He sat for another moment in a kind of trance, then
abruptly stood in a fluid, effortless motion that showed far
more strength than his small body looked capable of. "That,
then, is what you are here for: to help the new spirit of the
warriors for culture. To help us support the camps and
meetings and research and tools that is the heart of the Arms
of Vengeance. I know I can count on you. Wine and some
of our ancient delicacies will be served immediately. Thank
you all for coming."

As the throng surged and crowded forward to pledge their
support, to pull out checkbooks and sign checks, the young
boys filed quietly out at a single word from their older
leaders. Shelby bent and whispered to Carter.

"I'm going to check them out. Look around while I'm at
it. You hold the fort with Ramprasad."

Carter nodded, watched the boys leave, and thought
about Rip Ramprasad's speech. On the surface it
sounded harmless enough. What could be wrong with
teaching the young about their heritage, with wanting to
bring back the glories of the past? *If* that was what Rip
Ramprasad and the Arms of Vengeance were really
talking about. But Carter had been there in Madrid when
warriors a lot older and deadlier had blown up the
museum, and in Dallas when the restaurant was demol-
ished. Warriors with medallions dedicated to Krishna the
Charioteer and his warrior, Arjuna.

And the Killmaster had heard speeches like this one
before, from generals and oligarchs and dictators who said
one thing but meant something else. The old ways, tradition, the glory of the past too often meant reaction,
stagnation, elitism. Ramprasad talked of fighting modern-
ism, commercialism, and welfarism. Such words had a way

of turning out to mean iron-fisted repression, stagnation, isolationism, and ruthless exploitation of the poor. The rule of the past, of tradition, too often turned out to mean the rule of the rich and powerful *for* the rich and powerful.

"Ah, Mr. Craig. What did you think of my words, of the small demonstration of our goals and operations?"

Rip Ramprasad stood behind Carter. On either side of him were two young women in saris carrying his glass of wine and his plate of delicacies. And behind them, watching Carter closely, was another European the Killmaster had not seen in the room before—but somehow was sure he had seen somewhere else before. A man who, when he saw Carter watching him, calmly turned his back and became engrossed in conversation with two gushing women in Western evening dresses. Carter looked down at Ramprasad.

"I'm not sure," he said. "It sounds exciting for India, but I'm not sure. Are all your camps and training for young boys like that?"

"For the most part. We do recruit a small cadre of older youths, as I'm sure you noticed."

"And when the boys are trained, what do they do?"

Ramprasad smiled. "What do the Boy Scouts do, Mr. Craig? One hopes they take what they have learned, the principles and responsibilities and knowledge, and use it in the adult world as they make their way in society. Call it the needs of culture."

"You compare those kids to the Boy Scouts?" Carter said.

"In a loose sense, with more emphasis on our ancient culture rather than crafts and camping. What would you compare our boys to, Mr. Craig?"

"I had the Hitler Youth more in mind."

The two women behind Ramprasad glared at Carter, and all those close enough to hear him turned and stared. There was a few gasps. Only Rip Ramprasad showed no reaction.

"I hardly see the connection, Mr. Craig," he said.

A small, slender, dark-eyed Indian woman in a pure white sari seemed to appear beside Carter. She spoke to Ramprasad.

"I do, Rip. Tell me, are all the recruits for your camps boys? Where do the girls go? *Kinder, Küche, Kirke,* Rip?"

"The place of women in our ancient culture is important and honorable, Delah," Ramprasad said firmly. "I am aware we do not agree on this point. But we do agree on Hindu India, do we not? Strong and powerful and ours once more?"

"Will you bring back *suttee,* Rip?" the woman, Delah, said.

"It has never gone, my dear. Not for true Hindu women. It is not something any government can decide, or even a priest, but only each individual. I for one honor a woman who cannot go on without her man."

"A new India must belong to us all," Delah said. "The slavery of women cannot return."

Throughout the room many women murmured angrily against the militant young woman, but many others nodded in agreement.

"There will be changes," Ramprasad said coldly, aware of the disagreement around him. "We are not fools to think the twenty-first century can be exactly like the first century. It is a matter of principles, of faith, of culture."

"I worry, Rip, that your principles and faith and culture have no place for women beyond the kitchen, bedroom, and nursery."

An angry female voice rose above the murmuring in the room. "When you have succeeded in those places, Delah Pram, then come and talk to the rest of us!"

Amid general laughter, the militant Delah Pram turned and stalked out of the room and the house. With her gone, the rest of the guests seemed to breathe more freely. Rip Ramprasad sighed, and nodded to Carter.

"Delah is perhaps an example of what happens when a culture is lost, when alien ideas come into a world where they have no true roots. I am sorry you find our boys' training not to your liking, Mr. Craig. I understand your confusion, but it comes from your lack of understanding of our culture. For us, the way of the warrior is not that of the conqueror, the invader, the destroyer. Rather it is a matter of pride, of honor, of total commitment to our Hindu heritage."

"Hitler said something pretty much like that," Carter said.

"Yes, and it is good to instill pride of culture, of race, into a people. It is noble to teach honor and loyalty and devotion to your own culture. Hitler did much to restore the pride of the German people. It was only later, the insane distortion of his culture, the stupidity of his mad aggression, the horror of his limited vision, that he became the monster who had to be stopped."

Before Carter could answer again, a gong sounded through the room. Musicians and dancers appeared in the same archway through which the militant boys had entered.

"Ah," Rip Ramprasad said. "It is time for entertainment. Are you familiar with our music and dances, Mr. Craig?"

Shelby appeared smiling beside them. "If he isn't, I shall enlighten him."

Carter glanced at the big agent. Shelby gave a faint shake of his head. He had found nothing of importance. Together they stood with Rip Ramprasad and watched the three musicians sit cross-legged with their instruments on a small platform in a corner of the room. As they began to play, twelve almost naked dancers in thin silks and exotic headdresses glided into the center of the open floor and began a series of traditional Hindu dances. The dancers were all women, the dances all sinuous, sensual, seductive.

"Our dances are at the heart of our heritage," Rip Ramprasad said as he watched the slender women twine and turn and sway. "Even our gods danced. Shiva the Dancer. Kali. How could a man not be moved by such beauty, such sensuality?"

"I'd like it more if I could dance with them," Carter said.

The small man seemed to shake his head angrily as he stared at the swaying hips, the enticing movements of the breasts. "A woman should never dance *with* a man, only *for* him!"

When the dance finally ended, the small host stood as if transported into another time, another age. Then he sighed. "I am sorry you have not been impressed by our goals, Mr. Craig. But—"

"Who said I wasn't impressed, Mr. Ramprasad?" Carter said quietly. "Sometimes one plays the devil's advocate to try to understand better, right? I'm not totally convinced of what you seem to be trying to do, but I like a lot of what I've seen and heard. Maybe we can find some areas of cooperation between your people and American interests in this part of the world."

"Cooperation? Ah, of that I am not at all convinced. For a single American, personally, perhaps. But for your country and its interests, that is another matter. You are, it would seem, committed closely to our former countrymen in Pakistan."

"Commitments can change," Carter said.

"If it is not too late, Mr. Craig." The small Indian studied Carter. "Still, I do not deny we might find support from America, public or private, something of value in the future. Would you care to inspect one of our boys' camps? Say, tomorrow morning? You could meet others in the Arms of Vengeance who are far more articulate than I, perhaps find your personal enthusiasm increased."

"I think," Carter said with a smile, "I would like that very much."

"And I," Shelby said. "You've never shown me your work up close, Rip."

"By all means. Then shall we say tomorrow? At dawn?"

"Where do we go?" Shelby asked.

"You will be picked up. Now I must see to my other guests. Enjoy the rest of the evening, gentlemen."

Alone, the two agents sipped wine, smiled at the other guests, watched the dancers, and spoke quietly to each other.

"What do you think, Carter?"

"I think we'd better watch our step tomorrow," Carter

said, then ate a kumquat stuffed with a very sweet almond paste. "I think he wants my supposed money, but he doesn't trust either of us worth a damn. He'll have someone watching our every move."

Shelby nodded slowly as their host circled the room accepting checks. From the number of checks already piled on a silken cloth, the Arms of Vengeance had done well this night.

In the secluded country house where the two agents had told their host they could be found, Carter waited until Shelby was asleep, then used the telephone and his codes. On the far end of the line the never-sleeping David Hawk listened to his report.

"Someone could be using the Arms of Vengeance for cover, Nick," his boss growled.

"It's possible, sir."

"You'll find out?"

"I'll find out. But something else. There was a man I know I've seen somewhere before." Carter described the European who had been watching him at the party. "He's not someone I know personally, but someone I've come across, seen a dossier on, something."

"That's the best you can do?"

"Sorry."

"Not good enough. It could be vital. Are you alone? Somewhere where you can be out of it briefly?"

"Hypnotism?"

"It's a try."

"Let's do it."

"You're on hold while I get the Svengali."

Hawk went off. Carter waited. There was something eerie, unreal, about waiting in a dim room in a country house surrounded by the lush subtropical vegetation of Calcutta, while half the world away in a Washington penthouse Hawk prepared to patch a hypnotist onto the line.

"Okay, Dr. Murphy is on. Clear your mind, Nick."

Carter made his mind a blank. The hypnotist's soothing voice began to lull him into a relaxed trance. He listened to

the insistent words, the soft sound, the repetition of phrases
and numbers that sank him deeper and deeper into . . .

. . . the snapping of fingers brought him alert, his
hand on Wilhelmina, his quick eyes searching the dim
room, his ears listening to the faint sounds in the thick
vegetation outside.

"You okay, Nick?"

Hawk's voice came quietly across the line.

"What did I tell you?"

A crisp voice, Dr. Murphy, answered, "Very little. No
name, no incident. You do know the man you saw, but you
don't appear to know him personally. He's in your general
knowledge, but all we could get from that stubborn subcon-
scious of yours was that the man is connected to some
menace, many deaths, a kind of amoral arrogance you
detest. He is dangerous, but not to you personally."

"That's it?" Carter said.

"That's it. Can I get back to sleep now, David?"

Hawk growled, and the doctor went off the line. Carter
could hear the gruff director of AXE chewing worriedly on
his foul black cigar. Hawk was uneasy; he hovered over his
agents like a mother hen.

"Not much help," Carter said quietly.

"No, and it could be more than just important tomorrow
when you go into their lair. Be careful. If you know that
man, it's odds on he knows you."

"I hope he has as much trouble placing me," Carter said
lightly.

"Be very careful tomorrow," Hawk said. "It could be a
trap all the way."

It wasn't something Carter needed to be told, and it
showed how concerned Hawk was this time. A basic rule of
intelligence work was never to go into a situation where a
major factor was unknown. But this time it had to be done.

"I'll be careful, sir."

"Good luck, then, Nick."

And Carter was alone in the dim light of the country
house in far-off Calcutta.

TEN

"No," she said, "we will all go in our vehicle. There are no exceptions."

Tall for an Indian, sleek in a black jump suit that could have been molded to the curves of her lean body, the young woman came for them in a dusty Land-Rover at the first tinge of dawn light across the vast and teeming land. Her long black hair was pulled back into a tight bun, and she carried a large black canvas handbag that could conceal almost anything. Her long-lashed brown eyes had surveyed them arrogantly when Shelby had suggested they follow her in his Bentley.

"And no weapons are permitted."

She motioned to the small, silent driver of the Land-Rover. He came forward and patted them both down as the woman watched. They had anticipated this, and had left their weapons in the house. All but Hugo up Carter's sleeve that even Shelby did not know about and the driver missed.

"Come," the woman said. "My name is Kala, I will be your guide throughout the day. You are to go nowhere without me. Is that understood?"

"Why such tight security for a training camp for a Hindu version of the Boy Scouts?" Carter asked.

"You misunderstand, Mr. Craig. It is not for secrecy, but for sacredness. There are many parts of our camps that cannot be entered by non-Hindus. It is a matter of religion. You will, I hope, grant us our religious rights?"

"Of course, my dear," Shelby said, and smiled. "And I must say we are honored to have so lovely and prominent a guide."

She looked sharply at Shelby. "You know me, Mr. Shelby?"

"Everyone knows Kala Shastri and her family. Wealth, intelligence, and public service are noticed by everyone."

"Wealth and public service belong to my father," Kala Shastri said coldly. "He is a Westernized democrat and a modernist. That is not the path for India."

"What is the path, Ms. Shastri?" Carter asked.

"The path of the *Upanishads,* of the *Bhagavad Gita,* of Arjuna the warrior. The path of the orderly Laws of Manu, where all people know where they belong and are happy in their place. Peace on earth, Mr. Craig, within the strength of our ancient culture."

"You, of course, are Brahman," Carter said.

"On the contrary," she announced, smiling. "I am *kshatrya*, the warrior caste that will lead us back to ourselves."

"At whose expense?"

"Only the exploiters, the imperialists, the invaders," Kala Shastri said, her voice suddenly fierce.

"And who will benefit, Kala?" Shelby asked. "For instance, will those people over there glory in this return to the past?"

The big man pointed beyond the Land-Rover to the sprawling slum of mud brick and board shacks they were now passing. The ramshackle dwellings stretched as far as the eye could see, so much humanity teeming through them that it looked like a gigantic ant's nest of mud and garbage.

The beautiful woman glanced toward the fetid slums, and shrugged.

"When the true culture of our nation is restored, those evils will disappear in the tranquillity of order. They have come into existence because people have left their proper places, their traditional homes, to seek modern riches in the cities brought to us by the English and the Moghuls before them. As Gandhi taught, peace and love and happiness are in simple labor, not in the modern and alien ambition to be more than your ancestors. That desire has brought only chaos and starvation to our lower classes. It isn't poverty that brings suffering, it is anarchy."

Shelby shook his head. "I am sure that message will fall on receptive ears, Kala. It has a rather authoritarian ring to it, don't you think?"

"Only the authority of truth, Mr. Shelby, of the divine order. That is what we must teach, restore."

Carter listened but said nothing. They were ideas he had heard too many times before, more explicit in Kala Shastri's words than in Rip Ramprasad's last night, but there was the same echo of tyranny. People with thoughts like that rarely stopped with teaching their ideas. There was something far more chilling in the young woman's views than a Boy Scout troop. As menacing and violent as bombs in museums and crowded restaurants.

By now they had left the slums and the city itself behind, and were driving through countryside as rural as where Shelby had his country house, but a lot more open. It was farmland, the fields stretching away on both sides of the narrow road. And soon after a fork, the Land-Rover taking the left branch into more forested land, the driver turned off into a dirt track that wound through the towering trees and vegetation to a locked solid-wood gate in a high wall that disappeared into the trees in both directions.

The driver honked. A short, two long, two short.

"Religious reasons?" Carter said.

"Isolation from intrusion is necessary for proper study," Kala Shastri said.

The gates swung open, and the Land-Rover drove through.

Both Carter and Shelby noted the four boys, all under twelve, who had opened the gates and now stood aside. Each boy was armed with an AK-47 advanced assault rifle.

"Arjuna in the twentieth century?" Carter asked.

"Of course," Kala Shastri replied.

They drove on.

Another mile along the road the trees abruptly began to thin out, and low wooden buildings in the style of ancient India began to appear on both sides of the road set in secluded groves. There were old-fashioned village wells with bathing and laundry washing troughs, outhouses, and in the center a large communal building with carved and decorated eaves and roof beams.

Nothing seemed to move among the silent buildings as the Land-Rover came to a slow stop in front of the large communal building. It all had the look of a remote boys' school, a center of meditation. Monastic. Tranquil and simple. Yet Carter sensed something menacing, a suppressed, unspeakable violence. He tried to place it, and looked at Shelby. The big man, too, was staring around with a frown.

"Come," Kala Shastri said.

Carter and Shelby climbed out, and the driver immediately backed away and drove off along the road that vanished among the trees. The two Westerners followed the slender woman in the black jump suit along a path beside the communal hall. Then Carter became aware of what was menacing, the suppressed violence.

The carvings on the communal buildings were all of the Hindu pantheon in violent, savage action. With swords raised and slashing. Beheading kneeling victims. Disemboweling figures that were clearly Moghul, Muslim troops. Hacking at what were obviously British soldiers. On all the buildings were wooden plaques with the same relief carvings. Shiva, Krishna, the warrior Arjuna, savaging their enemies. Kali dripping blood and flesh.

But more than even the carvings of the violent gods were the silent faces at the windows. Boys' faces. One or two in each building. Staring out at them solemn and unsmiling. Hate in their young eyes.

"In here," Kala Shastri said.

It was the second largest building in the secluded camp, a low wooden structure with the same violent, militant carvings of the Hindu pantheon and no windows. Inside, there was a single large room with mats on a bare floor, ropes hanging from the ceiling, and gymnastic equipment. A slim, muscular youth in his early twenties led a dozen of the silent young boys through violent exercises with wooden swords and padded armor that looked like a more stylized version of Japanese *kendo*. Half battle and half dance, unlike *kendo* this contest was done in grim silence. Only the heavy breathing of effort, the sudden grunts of blows given and taken, an occasional sharp cry of pain instantly hushed as if shameful. They all wore only white loincloths, even the instructor.

Kala Shastri stood with Carter and Shelby along the side of the room, her eyes shining as she watched the boys pounding away at each other.

"Look at them. So proud. So dedicated. They are the hope of all of us."

Shelby said, "They seem rather grim, my dear. Like little robots."

"Nothing at all like that!" Kala cried. "Can't you see the purity of soul shining from their eyes?"

What Carter saw was hate, but he said nothing about that as the muscular young instructor gave a sharp command. The boys all stopped. They gave a loud cry in unison— *"Prabhuda Bharata"*—and broke up into smaller groups to put away their wooden swords and padded armor and begin working on the gymnastic equipment. When all the kids were at work, the instructor walked to Kala and the two visitors. She introduced them.

"Mr. Shelby and Mr. Craig, this is Lal Bahadur, the leader of this camp. Mr. Shelby is a well-known Sanskrit

scholar and biographer of Girsha Ghosh, Lal, and Mr. Craig
is an American businessman interested in the Arms of
Vengeance."

The muscular young man inclined his head solemnly
toward Shelby. "I have heard of Mr. Shelby and his work,
also his past service to our country."

Shelby acknowledged the compliments with a return
bow, and Lal Bahadur turned to face Carter.

"Perhaps there is something about our program I can
explain to Mr. Craig."

"Do your students all board here?"

Bahadur nodded. "We think it essential they live the life
of the *Bhagavad Gita* uncontaminated by the modern
world."

"Where do you get them?"

"From all parts of our country, Mr. Craig, as far as the
overall program is concerned. Our young people are rest-
less, especially those from good families. The sons who see
little of value beyond grubbing for money these days, who
have little opportunity to grow in our partitioned, poverty-
stricken country that is still owned by Europeans and
threatened by the Chinese, the Soviets, the cancerous
growth of Islamic fundamentalism on all sides, and the
decadent secularism of the West."

Kala Shastri's eyes gleamed. "Yes! India must rise from
the humiliation we have lived in since the Moghul invasions!"

"Of course," Bahadur said, "most of our boys in this
particular camp are from West Bengal. We do very well in
West Bengal, which suffered among the worst from partition. Almost everyone in our better families lost something
they owned in East Bengal."

"Aren't your kids a little young to be concerned about all
that?" Carter asked. "I'd have thought they'd have to be a
lot older to get into the *India Awaken* stuff."

Kala Shastri stared at him. "You, too, understand Sanskrit, Mr. Craig? That is quite unusual for an American
businessman, isn't it?"

"Why do you think my company sent me here?" Carter said. "Why do you think I'm interested in India? And I still think your boys are pretty damn young to care about *Prabhuda Bharata—India Awaken.*"

Lal Bahadur spoke. "To change the direction of a culture, you must start with the very young. You have to bend the twig early to make the tree grow where you want it to grow."

"Right," Carter said, watching the two Indians. "You said you do well recruiting here in West Bengal, but this camp is almost empty. How come? Where are all these recruits?"

"I don't think—" Kala Shastri began angrily.

Lal Bahadur broke in, "You arrived at a time when most of our boys are on a field exercise. Only the most recent recruits are here now."

"Just bad luck we missed most of your troops," Carter said.

Bahadur smiled faintly. "It would seem so, Mr. Craig."

"Still," Shelby said, "we can look over the installation, eh? Get more of an idea of what the Arms of Vengeance is all about."

Outside, Kala Shastri led them back toward the large communal hall. As they walked through the warming morning, Carter stared at the violent and menacing carvings that hung everywhere.

"The idea I get," he said, "is that the Arms of Vengeance stands mostly for blood and violence, a fundamentalist revival as bad or worse than Khomeini's Iran."

"Really, Mr. Craig?" Lal Bahadur said. "What makes you think that?"

"The whole setup. The battle training. The emphasis on swords, weapons. The isolation. And above all the carvings of the Hindu gods you have all over this place. Violent and bloody gods, as savage and unforgiving as any Ayatollah."

Kala Shastri whirled in a fury on Carter. "Typical Western stupidity! American ignorance! How did such an ignorant culture become so powerful? Barbarians! You have no understanding at all of the needs and dynamics of Hindu India. Your Western humanist ego makes it impossible for you to comprehend the mind of the *Upanishads,* the *Bhagavad Gita.* You want to work with us? How could you possibly do that with the limitations of your Western mind?"

"Perhaps," Lal Bahadur said softly, "Mr. Craig is not what he seems to be. Perhaps he has lied to Rip Ramprasad to get here and examine our camp. He seems to be convinced that he is looking for something other than a simple center for the cultural training of young boys."

Shelby held up his cane. "Now, hold on. I assure you Mr. Craig is—"

Kala Shastri interrupted him coldly. "Your word is not very good at this moment, Mr. Shelby."

"Why would an American want to work with us?" Lal Bahadur said. "Give money to the cause of Hindu culture? Show interest in the enemies of its great ally, Pakistan? You have supported Muslim regimes too long, have allowed the Koran to run rampant over Asia even to the point of supplying Pakistan and others with the capability to have nuclear weapons to dominate us."

"What are you really doing here?" Kala Shastri demanded.

"Yes," Lal Bahadur echoed. "What is your purpose? Who are you really?"

"Now, listen—" Shelby began.

"No," Lal Bahadur snapped. He turned and shouted in Bengali, "Boys! Here! Now!"

From the nearest buildings, some ten youngsters now wearing paramilitary camouflage uniforms ran toward the four. Each boy carried an AK-47. They quickly surrounded Carter and Shelby who stood unarmed in front of Bahadur and Kala Shastri. There was nothing the Killmaster could do with only Hugo up his sleeve as a weapon.

"I think, Mr. Craig, or whoever you really are," Lal Bahadur said, "it is time for us to have a serious talk. Boys, take—"

He got no further.

A fusillade of withering fire cut him down like a scythe. Boys fell in their own blood.

"Down!" Kala Shastri screamed.

The unwounded boys, and Carter and Shelby, dropped flat to the dirt in the morning sunlight as another volley swept the open space from the shadows behind the communal hall.

ELEVEN

Pinned down, the Arms of Vengeance boys shook in fear with their heads buried in the dirt.

Kala Shastri lay flat, and struggled to pull a mini-Uzi from inside her large canvas handbag.

Another volley whined over their heads, and Carter could see the shadows of the unseen attackers moving forward along the sides of the hall. He crawled to one of the bleeding boys. The child grimaced in pain.

"Hang on, son," Carter said quietly, and took his AK-47.

The clip was full, the gun ready. Shelby had done the same, and now lay holding his own AK-47. They both squeezed off careful bursts of three, and brought down three of the attackers whose dying screams sent the others scurrying back to regroup.

"We're sitting ducks out here," Carter said. "We've got to get back into some cover."

"How?" Shelby grunted. "We're pinned down good."

Kala Shastri's voice was high at the edge of panic. "Lal is dead! They will kill us all!"

The militant woman and her boy soldiers weren't used to

99

real bullets and real blood. It seemed to Carter that they talked a better game than they could fight. It would be up to Carter and Shelby if any of them were going to survive.

"We need a diversion," Carter said as another volley kicked up dirt in front and around them. "They have to stand to fire down low enough to hit us. They haven't decided to risk it yet, but they will sooner or later if we don't break out of our position."

Two bolder attackers tried a dash out of cover for a closer building. Carter brought one down with a single shot. Shelby hammered the other in a long burst of the AK-47.

"How?" Kala Shastri wailed in a hoarse whisper. "There is no way! They—"

At that instant another group of the young boys came running in their oversized uniforms from the other direction. Carter saw his chance. He waited five seconds for the attackers to turn their weapons on the newcomers, then leaped up just as the enemy fired in the new direction.

"Now!" he yelled. "Up! Up! Run for the first building!" He was crouched and already running toward the nearest old-fashioned building. "Up! Up!"

Shelby was just behind him, and together they scooped up some of the frightened boys. Shelby pulled Kala Shastri after him. They almost reached the building before the attackers had time to recover and turn back to their original targets. With his sixth sense for danger, and his quick eyes that had been watching back over his shoulder as he ran, Carter sensed the instant of renewed fire.

"Down! *Everyone down!*"

They all sprawled to the dirt as the assailants sent another withering volley after them.

"Crawl!"

Moments later the survivors lay panting in the cover of the narrow building under the thick trees. There were six shivering boys, Kala Shastri, Shelby, and Carter. On the far side of the communal hall the second group of boys lay in a bloody heap strewn across the patches of sunlight and shadow under the tall trees. In the distance other boys seemed to be running away, or trying to reach Kala Shastri and the survivors. As Carter and Shelby watched for a sign of the attackers advancing, seven more of the armed boys managed to reach them.

"Look!" Shelby whispered.

Figures flitted through the shadows under the trees between the buildings on both sides of where they lay under cover.

"They're working around to get us in a cross fire," Carter said. "I count maybe ten of them left. Any guesses who they are, Ms. Shastri?"

"Muslims! Pakistani swine!" the slim woman snarled, her fierceness returning now that Carter had them under cover. "Your corrupt CIA behind them as usual. Perhaps Soviets or Chinese. They all hate us, fear that we will succeed in restoring India to its glory."

"That's quite a list of enemies for a Boy Scout troop," Carter said dryly.

Kala Shastri glared at the Killmaster, but said nothing more. Shelby was organizing the young boys into a perimeter defense to cover both ends of the building, making them use trees and boulders as cover to protect the rear. Carter watched the attackers move up on both sides to trap them, then crawled to Shelby where the big agent watched the rear. They talked low.

"Our only chance is a breakout," Carter whispered. "Once they get us circled it'll be too late."

"It takes a lot more training than those boys have to charge through a well-positioned enemy. They won't be much use for anything except defending where we are."

"If we stay, those guys'll just pick us off one at a time," Carter said. "Unless reinforcements show up."

"You think there are older soldiers of the Arms of Vengeance that they're hiding from us, don't you."

"I'm sure of it," Carter said. "Nothing else makes any sense. The question is, where are they?"

"It might not matter," Shelby said grimly. "They probably don't give a damn about us, and Kala and these kids are probably expendable. All fanatics have tunnel vision: they don't care about people or human lives."

"Then we've got to bust out."

Shelby nodded. "How?"

"Only one way. A diversion."

"I'll do it."

Carter shook his head. "Your bum foot makes you too slow, Phil, and you're the only one who can handle the kids and get them out safely."

Shelby said nothing. He knew Carter was right.

"The rear is still open. They'll expect us to try a break that way. But they won't have covered the front because the barracks blocks us. I'll take Kala, and fake a breakout to the rear. When you hear us open fire heavy, you take the kids and head the other way fast. Then round up all the rest of the kids you can and get inside that gym building with no windows. There aren't enough of them to rush a building with at most two doors and a lot of guns inside."

"Right," Shelby said.

Carter crawled to Kala Shastri and quickly explained his plan. There wasn't a lot of time before the attackers would close the rear escape. The slender woman paled, but nodded. She was scared: this was for real and the kids had to be saved.

"There are only ten of them left," Carter said. "We'll try to cut that down, but we've got to move now. Ready?"

Kala Shastri nodded.

"Shelby?"

"We're ready," the big agent said.

"Let's go, then," Carter rasped.

Shelby gathered all the boys near the left corner of the building, all still under cover and firing at the attackers to keep them away. The kids weren't good enough shots to hit much, but they kept the attackers busy and at a distance.

At the other corner, Carter watched the figures of the enemy move on either side of them, coming closer and closer together.

"Now!" he whispered to Kala Shastri.

They jumped up and, running low, raced toward the gap between the two arms of the encircling enemy. They were over halfway before the attackers saw them. Voices shouted in Urdu.

"There!"

"Breakout!"

A hail of fire sent Carter and Kala diving to the dirt. Kala had her little Uzi up, and Carter aimed the AK-47 at where the figures of the enemy moved under the trees.

Another hail of fire scorched over them.

There were sudden screams of pain from both sides of Carter and Kala. The attackers were hitting each other! Carter grinned; he'd counted on that. The firing stopped as a commanding voice cursed in Urdu and Punjabi.

"Pakistanis!" Kala hissed. "I told you!"

"You fire right. I'll aim left. Shoot low and slow—get their legs if nothing else. Go!"

They both sent bursts into the shadows and underbrush beneath the tall trees of the secluded camp. Grunts and thrashing told them the enemy had at least hit the dirt. In the distance behind them they heard Shelby and the boys running. There were no shots in the distance.

A woman's voice called out among the attackers. "They're escaping the other way, Ahmad! It's a trick!"

The commanding voice said, "Let them go. We have these two, that's good enough. Get them!"

"Up!" Carter whispered. "Run straight ahead!"

He and Kala Shastri jumped up and ran straight ahead. The attackers were caught again by surprise. Carter fired a short burst, bringing down two on the left. Kala got one on the right. The attackers dived for cover once more.

"We'll make it!" Kala Shastri cried.

Then the four dark-skinned figures in camouflage uniforms seemed to rise out of the ground directly in front of them. There had been more men covering the attackers' rear. Carter shot one. Kala raised the mini-Uzi. The three attackers stood their ground and opened fire. Kala Shastri was blown over backward in a shower of blood, her eyes turned up and dead before she hit the ground. A bullet grazed Carter's scalp and he fell forward, the AK-47 ready. The three soldiers all aimed at where he lay.

"No!"

The commanding voice boomed from behind Carter. The others were running up. Carter stumbled to his feet and charged the three men in front of him. Something slammed against his head from the rear. As he fell into darkness, he heard the voice of the leader once more.

"Don't touch him! The Hindu bitch is dead, but I want the Killmaster alive!"

Carter came awake in darkness, his hands tied, bouncing on the floor of some kind of truck. There were voices speaking lazily in Urdu all around him. The darkness was a bag tied over his head. He listened to the voices. Five or six men were talking about how brave they'd been, how many of the Hindus they had killed, and telling dirty jokes about the dead Kala Shastri.

Carter flexed his right forearm behind his back. Hugo was still up his sleeve. These people had missed it too. Amateurs all. He lay motionless and listened to the sounds of the truck and the myriad sounds on the road outside. The bouncing that had awakened him was all but gone. The truck seemed to roll smoothly on a good road. The noises of other vehicles, of bicycles and throngs of people, were all around them.

They were in Calcutta itself.

The truck drove for another ten minutes. It stopped and honked its horn. Carter heard heavy gates open, footsteps running. The truck drove a few yards and the gates closed. More feet ran near the truck, and hands picked him up and carried him to the rear. More hands grabbed him and carried him over cobblestones, up some steps, and inside a building that smelled of tea and cardamom seeds.

"Put him there." It was the same commanding voice.

Carter was seated in a chair, his hands untied, and then tied again behind the chair. They were hasty, under the eyes of the boss, and Carter was able to slip his wrists side by side as they tied. Later, when he crossed the wrists, the ropes would be loose. It gave him a small chance.

The hood was untied and pulled off.

"Mr. Nick Carter himself," the commanding voice said, gloating. "The invincible Killmaster is not so invincible."

Carter let his eyes open slowly. There was no glare. The room was dim with heavy shadows and a single overhead light above Carter's head. He couldn't see the walls, but they looked like wood. The floor was inlaid polished wood; the furniture seemed typically light European-style white wicker with colorful Indian throws.

"Would you like a drink of tea before we talk, Mr. Nick Carter?"

The tall, rangy man who sat facing him had a dark, angular face with a nose like a sword, and heavy, cruel eyes. A long scar was ragged on his left cheek. He wore a green turban, military camouflage fatigues with black boots, and a broad smile of dazzling white teeth.

Three armed men were ranged around the commander, and behind him almost hidden by the shadows, a heavyset white man in chinos leaned silent against the shadowy wall.

"We *will* talk, you understand. A soothing cup of good Pakistani tea might ease your voice, Killmaster."

The commander of the attackers was enjoying himself. Carter studied him, ran the face with its long scar through his mental computer, put the picture together with the name the woman had called out during the breakout—Ahmad. Carter then added the white man in the room.

"Ahmad Ali Jinnah," Carter said, "with his CIA watchdog. The Arms of Vengeance must be more important than I thought to rate the Pakistani secret service's ace commando and assassin."

The Pakistani's face twisted with anger. Then he caught himself, and glanced back at the CIA man. "You are strange people, you Americans. In my country those who serve the government think as one or they do not think at all."

The CIA man had a Texas accent. "Carter works for a

different office with different ideas. We call it democracy, Ahmad."

"Ah, I knew there was a good reason we do not like too much of your democracy, Burger."

"It has its problems," Burger said. "But we don't let democracy get in the way of doing the job. You and me, Ahmad, we got our job, and we got to do what we got to do. So you ask your questions and we'll find out where Mr. Carter stands and what we'd better do about him."

Ahmad Ali Jinnah nodded and, unsmiling now, turned back to Carter. "What were you doing in the Arms of Vengeance camp if you didn't think they were important? Why go there with that Shastri woman and the enigmatic Mr. Shelby?"

"To find out if they are important or not," Carter said.

"Why were you there shooting them up?"

The tall Pakistani leaned over angrily and slapped Carter across the face. "I will ask the questions, dog! What is your mission here? Who in America is interested in the Arms of Vengeance?"

"They're subversive, Carter," Burger said from the background. "Anti-American. Someone's sold you a load of crap."

"How are they anti-American?" Carter asked.

"I told you—" Ahmad was on his feet, glaring, when a man came running into the room and whispered urgently into his ear. The Pakistani commando scowled. "Watch him carefully, Abdullah. You two, and Burger, come with me. Hurry!"

Jinnah strode from the room with two of the soldiers and Burger behind him. Alone with Carter, the third armed man, Abdullah, held his assault rifle nervously. He sat watching Carter, his jumpy eyes so intent on the prisoner and his duty that he never heard the door open again behind him.

The woman who came in softly was a smaller version of the dead Kala Shastri. She wore a similar black jump suit, and her black hair was pulled back and tied softly at the nape of her slim neck. In her hand she held a lethal-looking blackjack. She sapped the guard once, caught his limp form expertly, and lowered his body to the floor.

She turned to Carter, a short, razor-sharp knife in her small hand, a finger to her full red lips to indicate silence. She hurried behind him and started to cut his ropes.

Carter suddenly reached up and caught her wrist, and twisted the knife from her hand. The instant Ahmad Ali Jinnah had left the room, the Killmaster had crossed his wrists and easily freed his hands. He stared into the fiery dark eyes of the woman, Hugo ready up his sleeve.

She stared back unflinching. "You *are* the Killmaster, aren't you?" she demanded in flawless English.

"Who are you?"

"My name is Nasrim. We must escape. Hurry."

Carter hesitated for a split second. Then he picked up her fallen knife, cut the ropes around his legs, stood, and nodded.

The woman smiled. "Tie the guard."

They tied and gagged the fallen guard with the ropes and his own clothes, and the woman hurried toward a door in a different wall. Carter grabbed the guard's rifle and followed her.

TWELVE

The door opened into a narrow back corridor that had at one time been the servants' passage to and from the kitchen and the rest of the house.

"Through here! Quickly!"

It was the large kitchen. The old-fashioned cooking stoves and sinks were shadowy and abandoned. The woman, Nasrim, stood at a rear window watching outside. It was dark now, and Carter could hear the sounds of the night city all around. The house was obviously in the heart of Calcutta, the former mansion of some British official or merchant built around a courtyard with a high wall to keep out the Indians.

"Come."

They went out into the dark courtyard, and silently down some steps into a narrow stone passage that had to lead to a rear gate. No one guarded the overgrown and rusted iron gate set in the high stone wall. It was almost invisible under the vegetation, and even if the Pakistanis who apparently used the building as a secret headquarters knew the gate was there, they probably considered it unopenable.

"Watch behind us."

Carter held the M-16 covering their rear. Nasrim produced a large key and opened the rusted padlock. The gate swung silently open on hinges well oiled under the apparent rust. The escape route was not a spur-of-the-moment arrangement to free Carter; it had been prepared over a long period of time.

"You must have infiltrated the group," Carter said. "Who for?"

"Does it matter, Killmaster? I know you, and I am helping you to escape."

"It matters," Carter said.

"Then we will talk when we get where we are going."

She slipped out into an empty back alley so narrow they had to move single file around angles and turns until it ended at another iron gate. The bustling night street of the city was through the gate.

"I have a car parked just outside the gate. They will be able to see us as we cross the sidewalk through the people if they are watching. To minimize the risk, I will go out first and get into the driver's seat. If they see me, they will think I am simply on some errand. That is, unless Ahmad himself saw me, but that is a risk we must take."

"What about back in the room?"

"Ahmad will not return for at least another fifteen minutes, and no one will miss Abdullah."

"After you're in the car, what do I do?"

"Wait until I start. Then slip out and around the rear of the car. The crowd should help cover you. The back door is unlocked. Open it, crawl in, and stay on the floor until we are around the first corner."

Carter nodded.

Nasrim opened the narrow alley gate and slipped out through the throngs of night people into a sleek Jaguar. Carter waited until she started the engine, then ran low among the passing Indians and around the car into the back seat. Nasrim screeched away at once, almost sideswiped three cars, and merged into the traffic. At the second corner, Carter sat up.

"Okay, let's hear the story."

"Not yet. When we reach the safe house."

"The hell with the safe house! There was one woman with Ahmad's killers at the Arms of Vengeance camp. That had to be you. A lot of innocent kids were killed, not to mention two adults I'm not sure yet were doing anything."

"You have to break eggs to do a job, Killmaster, and don't cry too long over Kala Shastri and Lal Bahadur. They had both done their share of killings, believe me. Kala was in Madrid and Dallas." She turned another corner, and seemed to be heading for the same rich suburb where Rip Ramprasad had his mansion. "You can't infiltrate a violent enemy and stand aside from the violence. Sometimes you must attack your friends. At least the Arms of Vengeance are no friends of ours."

"Who is us?"

"I work for India, Carter. The exact organization is not important."

"You're a Muslim."

"Not all Indian Muslims are in Pakistan, nor are they all anti-India or anti-Hindu. My name is Nasrim Khan. I am from here in West Bengal. The partition destroyed my family. I have hated the partition and Pakistan and now the horror of Bangladesh since I was a child."

Carter studied the back of her head. It was a well-shaped head, the thick black hair pulled back on the nape of her slim neck. She was small and young and exquisite, and she could be telling the truth. She had freed him from the Pakistanis who would certainly have killed him, and with the CIA's blessing if he was in the Company's way. They would apologize to Hawk later. And she had blown her cover to do it. Why would he be that important to India?

"Why save me? You lost your cover."

"I had my orders. Someone named Shelby got word to my superiors of what happened. They seem to have considered you important enough to break my cover."

"So you work for the Indian secret service."

She said nothing, but her slim back stiffened behind the wheel as if shocked that she had made some mistake, let him guess who she worked for.

"If you want to think so."

Before Carter could answer, Nasrim turned into the dark courtyard of a small Indian-style house almost hidden behind rows of thick palms near the banks of the Hooghly River, the mouth of the holy and mighty Ganges that flowed through Calcutta into the Bay of Bengal. She left the car in the courtyard and motioned for Carter to follow her inside.

Carter looked at the car.

Inside, Nasrim stood at the front window, watching the courtyard.

"It's a trap?" Carter asked.

"You don't think we just wanted to save you, do you? We expect Jinnah will manage to trail us. If he does, he will see the car, know you and I are here, and attack." She turned to face Carter. "Then he and his unit will be finished."

"Your people are in ambush?"

"Yes, but you won't see them."

Carter looked out. The car sat in plain sight, and would be like a beacon when the moon came up. He saw nothing else, not a hint of anyone in ambush. Nasrim drew the curtains.

"They would expect us to be holed up tight," she said. "You check the other rooms."

Carter nodded, left the dark living room with its sparse and delicate Indian furniture, and walked through the other rooms. There were only an Indian-style kitchen, a European bathroom, and two small bedrooms. He closed all the rattan shades and was leaving the larger bedroom when Nasrim appeared in the doorway. She smiled softly at him. She had taken off her black jump suit and stood before him in an emerald-green silk robe.

"It will take Ahmad hours to find us," she said.

Carter really looked at her for the first time. Her dark hair pulled back in a loose bun on her neck gave her a soft appearance. Small and slim, her posture was elegant and regal in the flowing green robe, her legs neat and well turned, long for her height. Her breasts swelled high, and she continued to smile at him.

"Perhaps we could find something pleasant to do," she said.

"You have anything special in mind?"

She walked slowly toward him.

"I have heard," she said, close to him now, "that the Killmaster is as accomplished in love as he is in war. Is that true, Mr. Nick Carter?"

On tiptoe, her body pressed against him, she raised her arms and snaked them softly around his neck.

"And I've heard that Indian women are the most subtle and exotic lovemakers on earth," he said.

She brushed her lips against his throat, lightly licked the hollow under his chin.

"That is Hindu women, Killmaster. We Muslims are not at all subtle. Perhaps exotic, but above all passionate, and I feel passion for you, Nick Carter. What do you feel?"

For answer, Carter picked her up like a feather and carried her to the low futon that lay in the center of the bedroom. His hands told him that under the silk robe she wore nothing else. Her hands dug into his hair, and her teeth bit his neck hard enough to draw blood. They fell onto the futon, her brown body squirming under him.

He pulled off the green robe. Her small hands clawed at his belt as she bit his ear, and she moaned as she pulled his pants down and threw them somewhere in the dark bedroom. There was nothing soft or slow or subtle about them now, a physical desire far more ancient than the *Kama Sutra* burning through them as their bodies entwined on the futon.

Naked at last, drenched in sweat in the hot Indian night, they locked in an embrace so tight there was no way to know where one of them ended and the other began. Carter pinned her arms to the futon, and her legs opened wide and clamped around Carter's neck. There were no sounds in the room beyond their breathing. No time and no place. Time

stood still and there was nothing in the world but the two
bodies sliding and twisting, first one and then the other on
top, at each side, under.

Then her legs slid down both sides of his body from his
neck to his hips. His hands held her ankles and spread her
as wide as the Indian sky, and she cried out.

"Now! Now!"

His mind a great blank, carried only on nerves and
muscles and desire, Carter thrust himself inside her. Again.
Again. As she cried out. Again. Again. Again.

A minute. An hour.

No way to know.

Thrust and reach in and in and in and her arms and legs
gripped and hammered and twisted and thrashed and the
sweat like oil all over the two bodies Carter could almost
see as if from a long distance and . . .

The blended final long cries faded slowly away into the
distance of the dark room where they came to consciousness
side by side watching the sky.

Another minute or hour.

She spoke from somewhere. "I am glad you were at the
Arms of Vengeance camp. I am glad I was commanded to
help you escape."

"So am I, Nasrim," Carter said.

In the dark room he lay beside her without moving. He
watched the ceiling over the futon. He still wore his shirt. In
their passion, she had not noticed, nor felt Hugo under the
sleeve. Carter touched the small tattoos on each swelling
breast—the Islamic crescent and star.

"I was surprised, really," she said lazily. "What could
the United States want with the Arms of Vengeance? We
know little about them ourselves."

"It won't work, Nasrim," Carter said.

He lay quietly in the darkness. She was silent a long
minute.

"What?" she said.

"I said it won't work. You're not with the Indian secret
service, and there's no ambush."

She raised up quickly on her elbow and stared down at him in the dimness of the bedroom. "What are you talking about, Nick? How can you think that after—"

"You're part of Ahmad Ali Jinnah's Pakistani commandos," Carter said. "It's all a trick to lull me, to make me trust you, to make me tell you what Jinnah wants to know."

"Liar!" She raged down at him. "You think I would do—"

"I think you would do anything for your country and your cause, Nasrim. There was something familiar about you. I remembered the full description of the docent who shot the curator at the Los Angeles museum. It was you, Nasrim. I remember Shelby telling me of the Pakistani agent, Nasrim Nasrullah Khan, with the Moslem crescent tattooed on her breasts."

For another second she stared down. Then she moved like lightning, clawing at the edge of the futon. Carter sat up and Hugo leaped out of the sleeve of his shirt into his hand. He pressed the point of the razor-sharp dagger into her slim throat. She froze with the little Walther PPK half raised from where it had been concealed under the edge of the futon.

"Drop it, Nasrim," Carter said quietly.

She dropped the Walther.

"I did wonder why you kept your shirt on. Ahmad missed the dagger?"

"You're all amateurs." Carter smiled in the dimness. "But even amateurs can be dangerous. I'm going to leave you now before Ahmad and his men arrive. Unless they're out there already."

"You know it's no use, Killmaster. Of course they are out there."

He was still smiling. "No, they wouldn't risk being seen. They wouldn't risk some mistake that would tip me off. They had complete confidence in your charms holding me as long as you want, and they're waiting somewhere for a signal from you. You had a gun stashed in the futon, which means you planned to end up on the futon. And you'll have some remote device to signal them. I'm going to knock you out and tie you up so you can't reach any signal until I'm long gone. Sorry."

She whirled, cutting her neck on Hugo's point but not even noticing. White-hot rage flowed all through her small, slim, tight body.

"You Western scum, I'll—"

His left hand held her by the throat. She gasped, her dark eyes bulging.

"Be quiet, and you won't be hurt. You tried a trick, it didn't work. That's all. We'll probably meet again, I hope in better circumstances." He kissed her, and smiled once more. "It was good, very good. I'm sorry we won't have a chance to do it again for a while."

With a movement so fast she never saw his hand move, the Killmaster released her throat and pressed her carotid artery until she lost consciousness. He quickly sheathed Hugo up his sleeve again, tore up her silk robe, tied her hand and foot, gagged her, and left her lying on the bed.

She would wake up soon, he knew, but by then he would be long gone.

THIRTEEN

Nick Carter stepped into the bombed-out house in the Calcutta suburb.

"I thought you'd make it," Philip Shelby said. "Who were they?"

"Ahmad Ali Jinnah and his Pakistani commandos," Carter said. "You got the kids away okay?"

"Most of them. I didn't get much thanks. The police showed up eventually and took us in. The parents met us at the police station and got their kids away fast. I had the distinct impression they were as mad at me as at the attackers—didn't want anyone looking into the Arms of Vengeance."

"What about the parents of the dead kids?"

"They seemed almost as proud of their children as they were upset."

"Fanatics."

"In spades," Shelby agreed. "And, as you suspected, it looks like there's a lot more than children involved."

"What's happened?"

"It'll take a while. You hungry?"

"Thirsty, but I could eat."

Shelby tapped a small gong. When his houseman appeared he asked him to bring the leftover dinner curry and some beers. After the food had come, and well-chilled Kingfisher and Taj Mahal beers, they sat in the cleaned-up part of his shattered living room while Shelby reported what he'd heard.

"It came through no more than an hour ago from Langley," the big agent said. "There was an incident two days ago up on the Chinese border. The original report said Indian border troops had made an incursion into Chinese territory, had been chased away after a brief firefight, and that the Chinese troops had then been ambushed right at the border with heavy losses. Beijing was livid, demanded an explanation, an apology, and reparations to the families of the soldiers killed."

Carter drank the strong Taj Mahal. "Routine. What's the kicker?"

Shelby drank. "The Indians said just as vigorously that no such thing happened, that none of their troops had crossed the border. They claimed they don't even *have* any units in that particular area, and they were just as livid over what they said had to be some kind of Chinese trick."

Carter leaned forward. "So?"

"It went on a day or so. The Chinese said they could show the world the bodies. The Indians said they could show the world none of their troops were ever close to the spot. It went on like that, very tense I might add, until early today when—"

"The Indians discovered there *were* Indian soldiers in the area," Carter said. "There was an ambush, but the soldiers seem to have acted on their own without New Delhi's knowledge."

Shelby nodded. "Delhi has apologized to Beijing, explained it was maverick soldiers, and agreed to pay the families. Now the Indian opposition is livid and is demanding Gandhi's resignation. They're calling for the defeat of the government as appeasers, and a full investigation of the incident."

"Which Delhi is resisting," Carter said, "because they can't identify the maverick soldiers, don't really know who they were."

"Right," Shelby said, nodding. "They can't even identify what unit of their army it was. In fact, it doesn't seem like any unit of the Indian army was involved at all. When they reached the scene, no Indian casualties had been left behind. They found nothing but a lot of dead and angry Chinese, and a couple of gold medallions with—"

"Krishna the Charioteer on one side, and Arjuna on the other," Carter growled. He stood up and began to pace the bombed room. "The Arms of Vengeance people were disguised as Indian troops to start an incident. That's probably where all the real soldiers of the organization from that camp were."

"Very probable," Shelby said.

"How does it stand now?"

"The Company thinks Delhi has Beijing mollified. The Chinese field commander in the area seems to have agreed that the Indian soldiers didn't act like any Indian regulars he's run into."

"But another such incident could cause a border explosion between India and China, or worse."

"I'd say any more would escalate dangerously, yes," Shelby agreed. The big agent found a pipe on a patched-up side table, lit it, and puffed. "You want to hear the topper?"

"Shoot."

"Besides the medallions, the Indians who went up there found that all the weapons used by the fake Indian troops were AK-47s! Most of them were brand-new, still with their Russian, not Chinese, markings."

Carter sat down again and sipped his beer, looking both grim and thoughtful.

"Meaning it looks like the Russians and India are together against the Chinese, but what it *really* tells us is that the Soviets are working with the Arms of Vengeance."

"Or the Arms of Vengeance wants people to think that."

"Where do we find out?"

"The Soviet embassy in Delhi, I'd say."

"Can we get in?"

"Piece of cake," Shelby said grinning.

"Then's let's get in."

The two agents finished their beers, went out to Shelby's old Bentley, and headed off for the airport.

The reception at the Soviet embassy in New Delhi was an intellectual affair in honor of a cultural delegation from the Uzbek and Kirghiz republics that was in India to study Hindu art. Shelby had gotten invitations for himself as a noted Sanskrit scholar, and for Mr. Collins of the United States, a patron of the arts.

The uniformed guards at the outer gate passed them through to the polite undersecretary at the door and on into the large and glittering main reception room with its portraits of Lenin and Gorbachev. Under a sparkling chandelier a large crowd of Indian and foreign notables, art experts, collectors and wealthy patrons mixed with each other, the suave embassy staff, and the solemn Uzbek and Kirghiz delegations in their ill-fitting suits.

"They'd do better to wear their native dress," Carter observed to Shelby as they took glasses of sweet Soviet champagne and some of the caviar canapés.

"The ambassador seems to think so," Shelby pointed out. "He's not here. The chargé d'affaires and the military attaché are doing the honors."

"That should make it easier for us to get into their records."

"It should. I think the best way—" The big agent stopped, his eyes on the staircase to the second floor. Carter looked.

A tall, elegant-looking man in a well-cut and expensive gray Western suit obviously tailored somewhere other than the Soviet Union, or by a very good Soviet tailor, had come down from the second floor. The ambassador was with him!

"Hormuzkavali," Shelby whispered. His voice was excited. "Oska Hormuzkavali, the new number two man in charge of external ethnic cultures and relations in the Kremlin. He's one of the youngest, fastest-rising men in Gorbachev's new lineup. If he's here, something's a lot more important than a bunch of Uzbek museum curators."

Carter studied the tall, slender man who was at most in his early forties. He had the universal Georgian big nose and thick, dark mustache. The full head of unruly dark hair, hooded eyes, and pale skin. A crisp white shirt and Western-style silk tie. He was talking and the ambassador was listening as they walked slowly down the stairs.

"External relations of any kind means KGB," Carter said.

"Of course," Shelby agreed. "But diplomatic KGB, and at his level that would mean policy making."

"Negotiations and commitments."

"Arms shipments to promising underground movements."

"Right," Carter said. "I'd like very much to have a little talk with Mr. Hormuzkavali about our friends at the Arms of Vengeance."

"Then we'll have to arrange such a talk." Shelby smiled grimly. "Come on."

The big agent limped massively through the crowded room toward where the dynamic young Soviet leader was now moving from one Uzbek and Kirghiz delegate to another, giving each a smile, a word, a pat on the back. The politician at work in any country. All smile and platitude and empty eyes thinking about something far removed from what he was doing.

Shelby pushed in brazenly. "Comrade Hormuzkavali! Here is the American art patron interested in Hindu art I told you about. Mr. Collins, Minister Hormuzkavali. I think Mr. Collins would like to discuss an idea of mutual benefit, Minister."

The Soviet leader seemed slightly dazed as he smiled at Shelby, then shook hands with Carter. He was in his public mode, and Shelby knew that he'd probably met a hundred new people the last few days and couldn't possibly remember them all or what they had talked about. The Georgian was safe and relaxed in his own embassy, would expect no danger here, and would certainly be interested in any talk of cooperation with what appeared to be a well-known, probably wealthy, American businessman.

"Certainly. Of course," Hormuzkavali said, nodding, still all surface, doing his public-relations job. "Talk to our undersecretary. I'm sure I have some time open tomorrow."

"I'm afraid Mr. Collins has to leave Delhi tomorrow. In fact, he flies to Moscow tomorrow to talk to Minister Rubashov. We thought if you could spare a half hour now he could get a better idea of how his proposal will be considered? Somewhere private?"

Inside, Carter grinned in admiration as he watched Shelby work on the ambitious Georgian. Rubashov was the main rival in the Kremlin of Hormuzkavali's immediate boss. It would get the Georgian a lot of Brownie points if he could tell his boss what the American and Rubashov were talking about. It was too great an opportunity for Hormuzkavali to miss.

"Well,"—he glanced at his elegant Western wristwatch—"I don't suppose I'll really be missed here. All right, come with me."

The tall Georgian led them through the room and up the stairs to the second floor. Carter noted that the ambassador and the military attaché both watched them curiously and more than a little suspiciously as the three disappeared into an upstairs corridor.

Suddenly, Carter stopped.

"Damn! Shelby, I've forgotten I have to report to Dallas right now. Stupid of me, Minister. Tell you what, Shelby knows all the details of what my consortium back home has in mind. You two go on and discuss it, and I'll join you in a few minutes."

Before either man could answer, Carter turned on his heel and walked rapidly back along the corridor and down the stairs to the main reception room again. There he pushed quickly through the crowd and stepped behind a tall potted palm from where he could watch the stairs unseen.

They came down the stairs together. From somewhere up on the private second floor of the embassy. Carter had seen them standing far back in the upstairs corridor in deep conversation, and that was why he had immediately made his excuses and left Shelby and the Georgian staring after him.

Rip Ramprasad, the wealthy Calcutta backer and fundraiser for the Arms of Vengeance, in full Hindu regalia— and Lalita Chatterjee in a low-cut white evening dress that showed off every lush curve of the body Carter remembered only too well from their night in Dallas!

Carter watched them descend the staircase, his mind racing with suspicion and questions. What business did the Arms of Vengeance backer have on the private second floor of the Soviet embassy? It proved, without having to locate any other evidence, or pump Oska Hormuzkavali, that the Arms of Vengeance did have a connection to the Soviet Union.

What was Lalita Chatterjee doing in the private area of the embassy? What was an Indian secret service agent doing with Rip Ramprasad? Was there a connection between the Arms of Vengeance and the Indian secret service? Or was she in deep cover?

There was only one way to find out.

Carter stepped out from behind the foliage and followed the two Indians through the crowded room. They moved slowly, stopping to talk to many people as they crossed the room. Carter now recognized many of the same people who had been at the Arms of Vengeance fund-raiser at Rip Ramprasad's Calcutta mansion. They did not pause to speak to any of the Uzbek and Kirghiz delegates; they were not at the party to do anything about art or culture.

Carter kept as far behind them as possible, until they finally reached the far side of the room near the wide glass doors out into the garden. There they stopped, and seemed to be in intimate conversation, Ramprasad's eyes staring into Lalita's beautiful face with an interest that wasn't at all businesslike, his hand tracing the rise of her breasts out of her low-cut gown.

The exotic Indian agent's dark eyes seemed to smolder at his touch. She leaned, kissed him lightly, then took his hand and led him out through the open doors. A smug smile of anticipation played over Ramprasad's face.

Carter noticed others in room watching them with small smiles. He slipped out into the dark garden after them.

They sat on a bench in a dark corner under a tall tree.

Sat and talked.

Intense, vehement, involved talk. And it wasn't love talk. They neither touched nor kissed. Wide apart on the bench. An intense discussion that made Rip Ramprasad get up and pace around the bench while Lalita Chatterjee lit a cigarette, smoked in tense agitation, glanced all around—and saw Carter!

The Indian woman froze for a split second.

Then she stood, and said something urgent to Ramprasad. The Arms of Vengeance backer nodded quickly, turned, and strode away from Carter and into the embassy.

Lalita Chatterjee hurried to where Carter stood.

"Follow me! Now!"

She almost ran ahead of him to a side gate in the embassy wall. Carter followed as she opened the locked gate and vanished into the night.

FOURTEEN

In the broad, clean, modern streets of New Delhi, Carter followed Lalita Chatterjee to where a small British Austin was parked a block from the Soviet embassy.

At the car she turned, held his head between her hands, and kissed him hard and long. Then she stepped back.

"What the hell were you doing in there?"

"What the hell were *you* doing in there with Rip Ramprasad?"

"Working, dammit!"

"So was I."

She watched him on the dark street. "The Arms of Vengeance?"

"You too?"

She nodded. "What did you get?"

"That they have to have a Soviet connection."

"I knew that before I went in."

"The Kalashnikovs at the border?"

"You've got pretty good sources. Is that all you have?"

"Until I got here."

"Hormuzkavali?"

"He's not here to look at statues of Shiva," Carter said dryly. "What else did you have before you got here?"

She watched Carter for a time in the quiet night of the modern city so different from most other Indian cities. Then she turned to the Austin.

"Get in."

Carter walked around and climbed into the passenger seat. Shelby would take care of himself. Lalita Chatterjee interested the Killmaster now more than a minor Kremlin official with an interest in getting closer to an enemy of both Pakistan and China. There was nothing unusual in that. The Soviet Union was supplying weapons to an organization of fanatic Hindus that had some reason for shooting up Chinese, and the answers would come from the fanatics, not from the Russians.

"Where are we going?" he asked.

"You'll see." She drove fast in the dark night, through Connaught Place and down one of the broad avenues. "After the bombing of the Star of India, I picked up the trail of the bombers, and followed them to London and then Madrid. Eventually the trail led me to Rip Ramprasad and the Arms of Vengeance. Rip led me to the Soviet arms connection. But Rip is a front man, Carter. He knows what the Arms of Vengeance stands for, knows what the goal is—a new India ruled by Hindus as it once was in what Rip and those like him think were the golden days. But he doesn't know exactly how they plan to achieve their goal, or who really runs them, or where the main center is. I'd hoped I might pick up some of that at the embassy."

"Did you?"

"No. Did you?"

"Not yet. I may have a man working on it."

"I do have a man working on it," Lalita said. "That's where we're going."

She was driving now out of New Delhi into the old city of Delhi itself. As they plunged into the serpentine streets of the ancient city, past the endless bazaars, she told the Killmaster about Sait Raju. "He's a pretty well known painter with a big interest in our Hindu heritage. He says that happened perhaps because he grew up in and around Delhi where the Moghuls dominated so much. He came to detest Muslim art, Muslim culture. Art has led to life, and now I'm pretty sure he is heavily involved with the Arms of Vengeance. But like Rip Ramprasad, I don't think he is fully aware of what their plans are. Only I know Sait has met with at least one of the main leaders, and he knows where they have a major center somewhere not far from Delhi."

"You think he'll tell you who and where?"

"That's what I'm banking on."

"You'll take me along?"

She smiled at him in the dark little Austin. "After Dallas, how can I refuse you anything?"

They drove on through Chandni Chowk past the Red Fort and on through the mass of vehicles, animals, and pedestrians in and around the great bazaar. After slowly twisting through the narrow side streets for another ten minutes, Lalita finally drove into a courtyard and parked. The building had been a single house once, but seemed to be divided into three dwellings now, with Sait Raju and his studio occupying the right wing.

"Ah, Miss Chatterjee, come in, come in."

Raju was a small, thick, fidgety little man with large, determined eyes that belied his appearance. He wore typical modern Hindu peasant clothing—an all-white *dhoti*, sandals, chains of religious amulets. He led them into his studio where almost pop-art acrylic paintings of the Hindu gods hung everywhere. There was a modern Western technique at work, applied to traditional Hindu subjects and mythology.

Raju waved them to cushions and offered tea heavily spiked with cardamom and other exotic spices. Lalita nodded to Carter as they all drank the hot tea.

"Mr. Carter here knows about the Kalashnikovs too, Sait," she said. "Tell him what you heard about the border incident, Nick."

Carter told Raju everything Shelby had reported from the CIA. The small artist seemed to grow paler and more agitated as the story went on. Finally, he leaped to his feet and paced the room, waving his thin arms.

"I wish the return of the great peace that passeth all understanding, the rule of love and order. I cannot believe that the Arms of Vengeance could be involved in such violence."

"I visited one of their camps for young boys, Mr. Raju," Carter said. "They train with weapons, cry *India Awaken,* are devoted to the triumph of the *kshatrya* caste, the warriors."

"Yes, yes, but that is all symbolic! We ask India to awaken from the modern delusion, from the violence of the Moghuls, from the godlessness of today. The *kshatrya* are the warriors of Krishna, of peace and order and light."

"With AK-47s?" Carter asked.

"No, never!" The little man paced in agitation. "What do you want of me, Lalita?"

"Take us to the headquarters you know. To the leader you spoke of. Have you gotten the exact location of the camp?"

Raju nodded slowly. "Yes. I said I wished to visit the great leader, the swami and scholar Govinda Das Gupta. To paint his noble countenance and offer my work to the cause. They are pleased, and have told me how to find the camp at Rishikesh."

"You'll take us, Sait?" Lalita said pleadingly.

The little artist paced, agonized. He did not want to lead them to the Arms of Vengeance, but he had been shaken by the report of the Soviet weapons used on the Chinese border. His eyes decided. "Yes, I will take you. It is a long drive. We should start as soon as possible."

"What is wrong with now?" Lalita Chatterjee said.

By dawn they were past Saharanpur and driving steadily northeast into the foothills of the Lesser Himalayas with the great crest of the Himalayas proper in the distance. Each took turns driving on the almost empty road, avoiding ox carts and people carrying great loads on their backs, while the others slept.

"Rishikesh," Sait Raju had told them, "is where the training camp is, near a great temple of Vishnu. It is past Dehra Dun and Tehri, with great Nanda Deva to guard it."

They reached the city of Dehra Dun before noon and drove on over the rugged road toward Tehri as the fields became forests of evergreen oak turning slowly into pines and firs, and the road began to climb steadily. Now the distant peaks of the great divide of the Himalayas was clear, and the isolated peaks even closer, with Nanda Deva dominating all. A mile beyond Tehri, Carter studied the rearview mirror.

"We've got some company."

Lalita and Raju turned to look behind them. A four-wheel military-type small truck was less than a quarter of a mile back. It was driving very fast for the rugged and twisting mountain road.

"I first saw it behind us long before Dehra Dun," Carter said. "Then at Tehri. It could be nothing, but it's been following us for a long time."

"We'd better find out," Lalita said.

"You think," Sait Raju said uneasily, "it is someone who is not friendly to us?"

"Our friends don't know we're out here," Lalita said. "Unless someone told them."

"I did not," Raju said.

Carter shook his head, and watched the mirror where the truck was gaining on them. It drove wildly and dangerously on the narrow, winding forest road.

"And I didn't," Lalita said. She stared back at the small truck drawing nearer every moment. "It isn't any Indian army vehicle. It has no markings."

"But . . . but . . ." Sait Raju stammered. "I'm sure I see guns."

There was no mistaking the gun barrels protruding from both sides of the small open truck. The road was winding even more now, and the forest had changed to almost all fir and pine, the slopes of the foothills steeper and rockier. Carter studied both sides. A stream ran in a deep bed to the right, the slope rose sharply into the dark conifer forest to the left.

"They'll expect us to go up into the forest for cover," Carter said. "At the next curve I'll pull to the left, but we'll get across to the right into the stream bed. You're armed, Lalita?"

She nodded, and pulled a short, lethal, British Enfield XM-70 from under the front seat.

"Any more?"

"Sait, lift up the rear seat."

The artist did, and drew out two AK-47s. Lalita handed one to Carter, and smiled at Sait Raju. "You keep the other, Sait. Do you know how to use it?"

Raju swallowed hard, but nodded. "I have done my military service."

"Good," Carter said. "Then hang on."

With a curve ahead, Carter stamped hard on the accelerator, skidded the Austin around the curve on two wheels, and screeched to a halt just off the left side of the road.

"Now! Out!"

They leaped out of the still rocking car and raced across the narrow road and down the bank above the stream almost fifty feet below.

"Stop!" Carter hissed. "Back up at the edge and cover the road."

They scrambled up to the edge of the road and lay watching.

The small truck careened around the corner, skidded and slewed across the road as it saw the parked Austin, and slammed on its brakes. Six armed men jumped out.

One of the men was Ahmad Ali Jinnah.

"Pakistanis!" Lalita breathed.

The armed commando who stood beside the Pakistani leader and pointed up the slope through the thick conifer forest was a woman.

"Nasrim Khan," Carter said softly.

"Ah," Lalita whispered in his ear. "I should have known you would find that one. Did you admire the tattoos?"

On the road, Ahmad Ali Jinnah barked orders in Urdu.

"Two of you stay hidden here with the vehicles. Watch for them to come back if they get by us. The rest of you come on. Be careful, that Carter is clever and dangerous."

"So is Lalita Chatterjee," Nasrim Khan said.

The other four men laughed. "For a woman, perhaps," one said.

"For anyone," Nasrim said.

"Nasrim is right, you fools," Jinnah snapped. "Don't underestimate the Chatterjee woman. Now, move!"

The four ran up the slope of the steep hill, short M-16-A1 carbines held at port, and vanished into the trees. The two left behind crouched down in the cover of the Austin.

In the bushes Carter swore. "We'll have to take them out before we can disable their truck and get on our way. Lalita, do you have a knife?"

"Yes, I—"

Raju suddenly whispered in a shaking voice. "Look! They have seen something."

The two men behind the Austin were staring at the road, and then looked up across the road to where Carter and the others watched them. They stood, pointed to the ground, and then whispered to each other. One shook his head. The other insisted. The first pointed up the slope. The second shook his head this time, then suddenly started running across the road straight toward where Carter, Lalita Chatterjee, and Sait Raju lay hidden.

The second Pakistani followed, as if afraid to be left alone.

"Carter!"

"No time! Take them!"

The two Pakistanis were almost to the edge of the stream bank.

Lalita and Carter rose out of the underbrush and squeezed off two short bursts each.

The commandos saw them, stumbled as they tried to dive

for the dirt, but were dead in their own spurting blood before they hit the road on their faces.

"Back across the road into the forest!" Carter cried. "Circle right!"

They were too late.

As they raced across the road up ahead of the two parked cars, Jinnah and Nasrim Khan came out of the trees to see what the shooting had been about. The other two Pakistanis appeared farther away behind Jinnah and the small woman.

Jinnah and Nasrim raked the road with bursts from their M-16 carbines.

Carter and Lalita reached the trees and cover.

Sait Raju, running more slowly behind them, didn't make it. The little artist went down, ripped across the chest as if by a giant sewing machine.

"Shit," Carter swore. He raked the road and the distant cars with a hail of fire that sent the Pakistanis scrambling for cover.

"We're almost out of ammunition," Lalita said. "Unless we can get to my car. I've got boxes in the trunk."

"They'll have to reload too. Let's take them now."

Without waiting for Lalita, Carter slipped silently among the trees closer and closer to the vehicles and the four Pakistani commandos hiding behind them. Somewhere behind him he thought he heard Lalita, but he couldn't be sure, as he worked his way around to where he had a clear shot at the two Pakistanis down behind their own truck.

He blew one away with the last rounds in his AK-47.

Ahmad Ali Jinnah and Nasrim Khan ran from the cover of the Austin to take Carter from the side.

A long burst from the British weapon belonging to Lalita Chatterjee sent them sprawling and scrambling on their bellies into the forest again.

The last of the other two suddenly charged straight at where Carter crouched in the shadowed forest, crying *"Al Allah Akbar!"* Wilhelmina was steady in Carter's hand as he waited until the man was almost on him, a sudden hope in his eyes. Then Carter fired and the 9mm parabellum slammed the man into the air to sprawl on his back.

Carter moved low to Lalita Chatterjee in the gloom under the thick pines. "They're up the slope maybe a hundred yards now, Nick. They'll wait for us to come to them."

"That'll take too long," Carter said. "We didn't come here to shoot up a few Pakistanis. They know it's two against two, and they won't move on us. Let's get to that camp."

"We'll need poor Sait. He's got the notes of where we're going."

"I'll get him, and you put the truck out of action. Move it fast before they know we're not coming after them."

Lalita silently slashed all four tires on the truck, than cut some wires in the engine. Carter carried the dead Sait Raju to the Austin and deposited him on the back seat.

Moments later they were again on their way to the camp of the Arms of Vengeance.

As they turned the first curve, they saw Ahmad Ali Jinnah and Nasrim Khan come slowly out on the road to stare after them.

FIFTEEN

The road forked twice in its steady climb toward Rishikesh, and they took the fork shown in the dead Sait Raju's directions. After the second fork, they stopped to bury the artist. Even if Ahmad Ali Jinnah and Nasrim Khan managed to fix their truck, they would not know which fork to follow.

"Unless they know about the Rishikesh camp," Lalita volunteered.

"No," Carter said. "They were tailing us, and moved in when they saw a chance. If they'd known where we were going, they'd have been ahead of us and ambushed us."

Lalita laid wildflowers on the grave when they finished. "All he wanted was a return to the peace and beauty of our ancient Vedic past," she said sadly. "Now he has his own peace. He was a good man, with a wonderful karma. Perhaps he will become one with the universe and not have to return."

They drove on along the narrow, climbing road, coming closer and closer to the Chinese border. A mile before the small town of Rishikesh, Raju's notes directed them off on an even narrower dirt road that was unmarked. Here, the Arms of Vengeance was not advertising its presence. When Raju's crudely drawn map showed they had less than half a mile to go before the encampment, they hid the Austin under thick overhanging trees.

"No sign of guards," Lalita said. "That's strange."

"Yeah," Carter grunted. "Ready?"

"Let's get goin', as you Yanks say."

They moved silently along each side of the road, close to the dense forest growth on either side, Carter ahead and Lalita some four yards behind so they couldn't be caught in the same cross fire.

The rifle lay at the side of the road another quarter of a mile in. An old Soviet AK-47. Its clip was empty.

"Barrel's cold," Lalita said. "It wasn't dropped too recently."

They found the first body another hundred yards along, an Indian dressed in unmarked British fatigues and a paratrooper's camouflage smock. A golden-yellow beret was still on his head, with a hat badge of Krishna the Charioteer. He was not a boy, and he had been shot in the chest at least four times.

"So much for Boy Scouts," Carter said grimly. "This must be a training base for the real soldiers of the Arms of Vengeance, and it looks as if there's been a firefight."

Lalita seemed pale. "Yes, and not too long ago. This man hasn't been dead very long."

"Sometime yesterday," Carter decided. "They won't still be here."

"You can't be sure, Nick."

As if to answer better than Carter could, there was a sudden sound somewhere ahead, like metal striking metal. They both crouched, waiting, but the sound did not come again. Carter nodded. They stood, and moved warily on.

They passed open training fields, obstacle courses, firing ranges, village and urban fighting installations, climbing walls, and a mock river crossing course. All were empty.

The buildings came into sight around a final curve in the narrow dirt road.

What was left of the buildings.

Carter counted what seemed to be ten long barracks buildings very like those in the Calcutta area camp, another large communal hall, a windowless gymnasium and physical training buildings, what had to be the armory missing in Calcutta, a vehicle repair shop, and one low headquarters and administration building that still flew the flag of Krishna in his chariot.

All the buildings had been blown up.

"My God," Lalita Chatterjee gasped.

Bodies lay everywhere. They had fallen in the grotesque positions of battle. Most wore the same unmarked British fatigues and paratrooper camouflage smocks long obsolete in the British service, the mustard-yellow berets with the Krishna badges. They were almost all in their early to late twenties, all Indians, all armed with Soviet-made AK-47s. There was no apparent order to where they lay, no visible line of defense.

"Caught by surprise," Carter muttered, analyzing the situation. "A dawn or evening attack when they were finished training, their guard down. It looks to me like whatever outer defenses or perimeter guard posts they had, if any, didn't do their job."

"Overwhelmed early by professionals?" Lalita suggested.

"Probably," Carter agreed, shaking his head almost angrily. "Just kids, really, thrown into a war they weren't equipped to handle! What a stupid waste."

Lalita's voice was quiet. "Perhaps they didn't think so, Nick. Perhaps they felt it was all worth it. A new India."

"That doesn't excuse whoever runs the Arms of Vengeance from stupid incompetence. If they want a war, they'd better get people who know what they're doing. A cadre can train the young men so they have some chance against real soldiers."

"Where do they find such people who will believe in what they are doing?"

Carter glanced at the beautiful young Indian agent, but he said nothing. They moved on among the bodies, hoping to find one survivor, but there was no one. It was only when they expanded their search to the perimeter of the hidden mountain camp that they found the first enemy body.

It lay almost entirely hidden in a narrow gulley under the tall pines that bordered the camp. They looked down at the dead man.

"Chinese," Lalita said.

Carter slid down into the gulley to bend over the dead Chinese. The soldier wore a one-piece green jump suit and a soft-ribbed black helmet, and carried a Type 81 assault rifle with a seventy-five-round drum. Carter looked up at Lalita.

"Elite paratrooper, dropped in for a fast raid. The Arms of Vengeance didn't have a chance."

"He was the only casualty?"

Carter shook his head. "They carried off their dead and wounded. That's standard in a strike they don't want known, and an operation inside Indian territory would be something they certainly wouldn't want known, no matter what the reason. They just missed this guy because he was almost hidden in the gulley, and they may have been at the limit of their operational time schedule."

"Why, Nick?"

"Why the attack? Probably because of the border incident and ambush. Either Chinese intelligence or recon located where the ambushers were from, and then the paratroopers came in to clean them out. If Delhi really didn't know who the ambushers were, the whole thing might never come out. If Delhi *did* know, after denying it they couldn't say anything."

"What do we do?"

"Let's go over the whole place and see if we can find a lead to the AV's real main headquarters or another training camp."

"All right, I'll—"

This time the sudden sound was unmistakable.

The snapping of twigs, a slow, heavy running somewhere in the camp as if the runner were injured.

"Down!"

Lalita flopped on her back and slid down into the gulley with Carter. They scrambled back up to the rim, one on each side, weapons ready.

Listened.

There was silence.

Then the sound of movement, slow and careful, among the bombed buildings. The click of metal. It was impossible to tell exactly where the sounds were coming from, or how many were making the sounds. But it couldn't be a lot of people.

"More than one," Carter whispered, "but not too many. Maybe three or four."

"Chinese?"

"At least one sounds wounded. They could be some of the Chinese injured and separated and left behind, or it could be survivors of the Arms of Vengeance people."

"What do we do, Nick?"

"Wait."

They waited.

There were no more sounds. Just silence and the cries of birds. A scurrying of small animals somewhere among the towering pines.

An hour passed.

The Killmaster studied every inch of the camp that faced them. There were two long barracks, both shattered but with one wall of each still standing. Between them was open space leading back to the destroyed communal hall, the bodies of the Arms of Vengeance soldiers piled everywhere and beginning to rot even in the cool mountain air. On either side of the long barracks buildings were smaller storage sheds that had not been destroyed, probably because no one had taken cover there, and the attacking Chinese paratroopers wanted to carry away anything of value in them. Then the forest closed in on both sides of the small storage sheds.

"What is happening, Nick?" Lalita asked, wide-eyed. "Perhaps they are too injured to continue? Or dead?"

"Or they're waiting for us," Carter said. "That means no more than two of them also. They don't feel strong enough to move on us."

"What do we do?"

"We move on them."

"But we don't know where they are! They would have all the advantage."

"We'll find out where they are," Carter said. "At least one is wounded, and that's our advantage. Ready?"

"As I'll ever be," she said grimly. "We circle through the forest, get behind them?"

"That's what they'll expect, so let's go straight at them instead."

She nodded. Carter gave the signal.

They slipped up and over the edge of the gulley that faced the long, gutted barracks directly in front of them. Weapons cradled in their arms, they crawled rapidly across the twenty yards of open space.

No one fired at them.

Inside the bombed ruin, they crouched low in the shelter of the wall that was still standing, then moved rapidly on toward the corner.

The big man in gray coveralls jumped around the corner, balancing on his one good leg.

"Nick!" Lalita cried.

The Type 81 assault rifle with its round drum swung straight at Carter and Lalita Chatterjee.

Carter's finger tightened on his trigger.

But he didn't shoot.

"Should have known," Philip Shelby said. He lowered his Chinese weapon and limped forward on his cast.

"How the hell did you get here?" Carter demanded.

"A little indiscreet talk by the ambitious Oska Hormuz-kavali who was too eager to know what the American millionaire had to offer, and maybe get a piece of the action for his department," Shelby said. "Plus some snooping in the embassy files while Mr. Hormuzkavali took an unexpected nap. What I got led me straight here where the last shipment of Kalashnikovs came. How did you manage it?"

Carter told him of Lalita Chatterjee's infiltration and connection to Sait Raju. "We were held up by Ahmad Ali Jinnah and his crew. Did you get here in time to see the attack?"

Shelby shook his head.

"Our Chinese friends were long gone with their dead and wounded by the time I made it. But I did come up with a catch."

The big agent limped back around the charred corner of the building wall. He returned with a small, unimposing Indian with rimless eyeglasses. The little man was resplendent in the gold-frogged tunic, narrow gold trousers, gold sandals, and gold turban of a maharajah. The little peacock of a man glared up at the giant Shelby who was holding him by the scruff of the elegant tunic like a small dog.

"Who is he?" Carter asked, staring at the regally dressed Indian. "Where'd you find him?"

The small man glared from Shelby to Carter, and then saw Lalita Chatterjee. His sharp black eyes snapped as they looked at the beautiful Indian agent, then glared back at Carter.

"I demand to be released at once!"

Shelby shook the little man like a rag doll. "I'll turn you loose when you tell me who the hell you are and what you were doing holed up in that bunker."

"Bunker?" Carter said.

"Tucked in all snug," Shelby said. "I searched the whole place for survivors and found one guy barely alive who kept saying, 'The temple . . . the temple.' So I looked all over and finally found a small temple to Krishna up the mountainside from the main camp. There were bodies all around it as if there'd been one hell of a fight to defend it. Lots of evidence the Chinese didn't get off too easy either.

"So I went inside and looked all around. I couldn't find anything special, just the usual statues and incense and flowers. Then I heard this tapping. When I found where it came from, I heard a faint voice under the incense and offerings table. The table moved when it was pushed hard, and there was a trapdoor under it. When I opened it, there was our friend, scared to death and damned mad at the same time."

The little man fumed, "This atrocity must be reported! I must go to—"

Shelby ignored the irate Indian. "Obviously he's some kind of honcho they were ready to die to protect, so maybe we'd better take him to Delhi and turn him over to Indian intelligence."

The small man suddenly became silent. Carter looked at him, and then at Shelby.

"I don't think he wants to go to Delhi, you know?"

"I don't think he does," Shelby agreed.

"What do you think, Lalita?"

Carter turned to the Indian agent. She stood with her lethal Enfield XM-70 aimed straight at Carter and Shelby.

"I think we will go wherever Master Govinda wants to go."

"What the—!" Shelby sputtered.

"So?" Carter said. "Manuela Torres was right after all. The return to Hindu Mother India?"

"Manuela always was observant," Lalita said. "Take their guns, please, swami."

"No," Carter said. "It's a standoff, Lalita. You can't get us both without one of us getting you or your guru there."

Lalita smiled thinly. "Look around you, Killmaster."

Carter and Shelby looked behind them. They looked left and right. The youths in camouflage smocks and yellow berets stood all around them, AK-47s leveled.

SIXTEEN

The small Hindu motioned imperiously, and two of the Arms of Vengeance men came to take Carter's and Shelby's weapons. There were no more than eight of them who had come up silently while Carter and Shelby were preoccupied with the gaudily dressed swami. They were all in their early twenties. Carter surrendered his borrowed assault rifle, and let the solemn youths find Wilhelmina. They missed Hugo and Pierre.

Carter smiled at Lalita. "Hidden transmitter?"

"Warning signal in the Austin," she said. "I expected someone to spot it, but when we found the camp destroyed I didn't think anyone would."

"Fortunately," the little well-dressed Hindu said, "these boys returned for me. They were on a mission when the Chinese attack came, but knew that if there were any way at all, our brave men would have protected me to the end."

"Then you have to be Govinda Das Gupta," Carter said.

"Das Gupta!" Philip Shelby exclaimed. "Not the great Govinda Das Gupta of Oxford and Harvard?"

The little man preened slightly. "I have had the honor to

143

teach at those institutions, Mr. Shelby, and your fame has not escaped me. I only wonder why you have not yet joined us."

"I'm a scholar, Master Govinda, not an activist."

"There comes a time, Mr. Shelby, to stop thinking and act. I, too, am not by nature a man of action, but I heard the cry of sorrow of my people, and the call to action had to be answered."

"Teacher of what?" Carter asked.

"Master Govinda is the greatest living Sanskrit scholar, Nick," Shelby explained. "He's spent most of his life teaching in the West. A scholar of language, of culture, and of Hindu history and philosophy. He *is* India to most of us in the field."

Govinda Das Gupta's eyes shined with a white heat. "And to all my countrymen perhaps one day! When India has awakened and we all live in a new, pure, benevolent India. The time has passed for scholarship and history. We must now make our own history into the great vedic civilization it once was and will be again."

The small man waved his arms, his voice mesmerizing Lalita Chatterjee and the young militants around them. "Look at this atrocity! I can accept war for the great cause of ending all war. But in truth war is no longer a civilized option for the world and that is why we must cleanse first India and then perhaps the world. If we do not act, by the Western year of 2020 India will have the distinction of being the most populous country the world has ever known, and at the same time the most bloody, backward, confrontatious, and death-prone."

His fierce eyes looked around at the charred ruins, and at them all. "What a repulsive, grisly distinction! Unless we return to the spiritual sources of our true history, to the transcendental peace and tranquillity that is the core of our gift to humanity, we will die in a sea of blood and drag the rest of this world down with us."

Carter saw the burning fanaticism in the small man's dark eyes, the response on the almost trancelike faces of the young Arms of Vengeance soldiers. Even Lalita Chatterjee was transfixed with the vision of the small man's words, hope and belief like a flame in her eyes.

"And," Carter said, "you're going to achieve this paradise on earth with armed soldiers and bloody battles?"

"Not paradise on earth, Mr. Carter!" Das Gupta said hotly. "That is the error Westerners always make. Westerners—Muslims, Jews, Christians—have no understanding. That is why we must force them to see, to open their eyes. India will awaken, and lead the world to awaken. On earth there is only the path of peace and tranquillity toward the ultimate paradise of oneness with the universe. It is the correct path we will restore before we all are drowned in the sea of blood and error."

"You can't do it with guns, Master Govinda," Shelby said.

"There is no other way! The path of the warrior must lead to the path of understanding. It is so written. Gentlemen, I know how hard it is for the West, but join us and see. Come to our center and see our purity."

"Guns won't do it, Das Gupta," Carter said. "You don't have enough, and you never will. Even if you start a war between China and India, it won't be your path that comes out the winner. You're crazy if you think so, letting your fanatic dreams hide reality."

Now Govinda Das Gupta smiled. It was an almost insane smile, cunning and triumphant at the same time. "Ah, but I do not think I am so crazy, Mr. Carter. I think it is time to show you what we really can do."

He barked an order in Hindi, and the soldiers and Lalita Chatterjee began to march Carter and Shelby through the destroyed camp and back along the road to where an open personnel carrier stood beside Lalita's Austin. They were herded into the carrier, and Govinda Das Gupta smiled up at them.

"I think a visit to our holy city of Kamarpuri is what you need for your spiritual rebirth, gentlemen. We will talk again by the waters that feed the sacred Ganges."

The canvas sides were lowered on the carrier, the rear flap dropped, and the vehicle moved off with Shelby and Carter blind prisoners inside.

By the angle of light through the gaps in the canvas, Carter knew they had moved south and east in the direction of Lucknow. Far ahead, down the Ghaghra and the Ganges itself, lay Calcutta. They passed through many towns and even cities. By the time the rear flap was flung open, it was dark outside.

"Kamarpuri for sure," Shelby said. "It's on the Ghaghra, one of the main tributaries of the Ganges. Less holy than Varanasi or Allahabad, but particularly devoted to Krishna the Charioteer."

"The warrior again," Carter said. "Our Master Govinda doesn't seem to be able to decide what he wants to be—a god or a warrior."

"Both," Shelby said. "That's the problem. Govinda, and maybe most young and wealthy Hindus want to rule as Hindus, but they are tired of being pushed around by Europeans and Muslims. They want to beat the shit out of them as warriors too."

"The warrior-god who will lead to the path of peace and eventual oneness with the universe," Carter said. "One hell of a powerful message, and not just for Hindus or Buddhists."

"If it ever got a real start," Shelby added, "it could go anywhere."

"Then we'll make sure it doesn't get a start," Carter growled.

But that looked a lot easier to say then to do as the two agents were ordered out of the personnel carrier and found themselves in the stone courtyard of a massive stone temple with lots of towers and walls over fifty feet high. The single entrance they could see was through a long tunnel with an iron gate at each end. More armed youths of the Arms of Vengeance stood guard all around the courtyard.

Govinda Das Gupta was nowhere to be seen, but Lalita

Chatterjee had parked her Austin behind the carrier and walked toward the two captives.

"Come inside, Nick, Mr. Shelby," she said. "We want to convince you that we mean no harm to anyone except the killers and exploiters and tyrants of this world."

"That, Miss Chatterjee, is what every tyrant since time began has said," Shelby said.

Carter listened. He heard no sounds of city streets outside the high walls. None of the noises of people. Only trees rustling, and underneath everything the running of a large river close by.

"You are wrong, Mr. Shelby," Lalita said quietly. "Master Govinda and his disciples want only a return to the path of tranquillity led by our Hindu philosophy and its way of life for the world."

"Anyone who knows what is good for the whole world, Lalita, is a fanatic," Carter said. "How did you get mixed up with this Govinda Das Gupta?"

"How, Nick? Or why? How doesn't matter, only why. I got involved, as you say, by seeing the corruption, the self-interest, the self-serving, all around me in our government and those of most of the world, communist or capitalist, superpower or third world. I've worked all my life for India, and I suddenly saw that there is no India to work for. There are no values, only advantages. No purposes except to grab for yourself, person or nation. No concern for anything but power and money. I saw that women are nothing, that even in our most advanced countries women are still not equal and never will be. Master Govinda teaches that men and women are one, that the vedic path of peace and purity and selflessness is the way of both and of the world."

As Carter listened, he realized that Govinda Das Gupta was a powerful, almost hypnotic force who could reach even the brightest, most educated, and Westernized of Indians. If he could hit a need in Lalita, and subvert her from her work in the Indian secret service, from her devotion to her country, he could reach anyone.

"The problem we agree on," Philip Shelby said. "It's your solution that worries me."

Lalita smiled, almost eagerly. "It will not for long. Not when you see what we can do. Now, please come with me."

She took the two men into the temple with its large bare room for devotions. Offerings of flowers and fruits were piled before the statues of Krishna and Brahma and Vishnu, and the heavy odor of burning incense hovered everywhere. But Lalita led them on across and through a door into the living quarters of the temple.

They moved through the ancient stone corridors, lined with silk and wool wall hangings, and up an endless flight of stone stairs to a small room at the top of a tower. She nodded them inside. It was a small, bare room with a few mats and cushions, a toilet, and a single narrow window high up through which they could see a few stars.

"Perhaps when you understand more, we can give you better quarters," the beautiful woman said gravely. "For now, Master Govinda does not feel he can risk an attempt to escape and perhaps bring our enemies against us."

They heard the lock turn as she left, then both looked slowly around the stone room.

"There's always a way out," Carter said. "Sometimes it takes too long to find it."

"Besides," Shelby said lightly. "We want to see what Lalita and Das Gupta want to show us, don't we?"

Carter nodded. "That we do. So, now, I suggest we sleep. I don't know about you, but for me it's been a long day."

The two agents lay on the mats and cushions and promptly fell asleep.

The great steel vessel with its strange blue light in the water-filled tank towered over Carter and Shelby. There was little sound beyond a low hum and the click and beep of instruments, an occasional hiss of steam and clang of a metal cover or valve.

The two white-smocked women who sat at the control

console stood when Lalita and Govinda Das Gupta led Carter and Philip Shelby into the vast room under the temple above.

The women were both small and dark. One was in her mid-forties, the other younger. When they spoke, it was in good English but with accents that Carter immediately identified. The women were Cubans. They spoke to Das Gupta, but seemed to be strongly aware of the sixth person in the spotless air-conditioned room.

He stood half in shadow to the left as Carter and Shelby came in, and at first the Killmaster barely looked at him. It was the machine, the complex of jacketed vessels, pipes, gauges, dials, and electronics. He knew what it was instantly, and whirled on Das Gupta who was staring proudly at the installation.

"This is what you're so proud of?"

"You are impressed, Mr. Carter. So you should be. You see, we in the Arms of Vengeance are not simple fanatics playing our foolish little games you oh-so-arrogant Westerners and Orientals can brush away. You will have to deal with us."

Carter stared at the preening little man.

Shelby said, "What is this thing, Carter?"

"It's a nuclear breeder reactor, that's what it is. It makes plutonium, and plutonium is really only useful in bombs."

It was Shelby's turn to stare at Das Gupta. "You're insane!"

Das Gupta's eyes blazed. "No, it is the world that is insane! When they know we too can play their mad game they will destroy all their weapons and we can all live in peace."

"No one builds a plutonium reactor for peace," Carter said. He watched the little Hindu narrowly. "This isn't your technology." He looked at the two Cuban women. "It isn't even Cuban technology. No, it's someone else. Who?"

"Very intelligent, Mr. Carter. I have heard much of the Killmaster of AXE, and most of it seems to be true."

They all turned to look at the sixth man who stepped out

of the shadows. He was the same man Carter had been sure he knew but couldn't place at the fund-raising party at Rip Ramprasad's house in Calcutta. Now he wore simple black coveralls like a German World War II tank commander, and as he smiled thinly at Carter, the Killmaster suddenly placed him. It was the context of the breeder reactor and its technology that jarred the memory loose.

"Herr Doctor Professor Georg Gillet," Carter said. "No wonder I couldn't bring up the name and connection. It's hard to remember a dead man when you see a live one."

Georg Gillet shrugged. "It was necessary for me to 'die' if I were to properly continue my work in a manner that would be appreciated."

Both Shelby and Lalita Chatterjee were watching Carter and the stranger. It was Shelby who asked.

"Who is he, Nick? What's this all about?"

"Dr. Georg Gillet, son of the great German physicist Max Gillet, who almost developed the nuclear bomb in World War Two before we did. If the Nazis hadn't been so stupid and lost all their Jewish physicists, and a great many more who wanted nothing to do with the Nazis' 'arranged' science, Max Gillet and the others would have beaten us. After the war he and Georg came to the States. Georg was already a nuclear physicist, and went on to become one of the world's best."

"I remember now," Shelby said. "He had some arguments with the Atomic Energy Commission, didn't he?"

"And with the Pentagon and the White House. He found the States far too conservative in our attitudes toward nuclear power and weapons. He heavily favored tactical atomic weapons."

"It was the only proper position," Georg Gillet raged, "the only realistic recognition of facts, but the stupid Americans were too afraid to face reality. The bomb, tactical weapons, *will* be used, and it is only a matter of who uses them first and best. This talk of no one winning a nuclear war is stupidity. Someone will win, and survive, and rule the world. You Americans are afraid of this truth, but would never have let me go. It was therefore necessary to 'die' and disappear."

"To the Arms of Vengeance?" Carter asked.

Gillet smiled. "To those who know what to do with power, Mr. Carter. The three superpowers are so bloated with success they can no longer think or act. We will set them at each other's throats, make India ours, and, when it is time, the whole world!"

Carter looked at Govinda Das Gupta and Lalita Chatterjee. "The path of peace and tranquillity? It doesn't sound like Gillet and his Cubans have much peace and tranquillity in mind."

"Dr. Gillet means India and the world will follow our teachings, and there will be a oneness with the universe, Nick," Lalita said. "We will use nuclear power for the good of the world, not for our own gain as you and the Soviets and Chinese do now."

Govinda Das Gupta looked a little uneasy. "Professor Gillet speaks in the Western language of violence, Mr. Carter. He will see the strength of love as he works with our cause, and then he will see the true path."

"Why," Carter said, "do I feel someone is fooling himself around here, Das Gupta? And I don't mean Gillet. Max Gillet was a brilliant scientist—and a dedicated Nazi. I think Georg there is a chip off the old block, and you'll end up with damn little peace or tranquillity when he gets his plutonium bomb and your soldiers to deliver it."

"Shut your stupid mouth, Carter!" Gillet snarled.

"Someone is using someone here, and I don't think it's you, Das Gupta."

Gillet stalked forward, the two Cuban women scientists behind him. "I told you there was no way to reach him, Das Gupta. They must both be killed at once!"

SEVENTEEN

Govinda Das Gupta and Lalita Chatterjee were horrified.

"To kill in battle for the truth and the path to universal peace is honorable, Dr. Gillet, but we do not kill in cold blood. That is the way of violence, of our enemies."

Gillet shook his head angrily. "We are so close to success, Master Govinda. To the mastery of India and one day a totally peaceful world. These men do not understand your vision, and they are extremely dangerous. Carter has the power of the United States behind him, and Mr. Shelby is much more than he seems. He works for the CIA, for MI5, and for the Indian secret service." The renegade German-American looked at Lalita. "You did not even know that, did you, Miss Chatterjee? You own people hide such important facts from you. Can we trust any of them?"

Lalita blinked at Shelby, then looked back at Gillet. "What do we gain by executing them, Dr. Gillet? What danger are they to us now?"

"Alive they can always escape, Miss Chatterjee. Dead they can do us no harm. I must insist we protect our work."

Govinda Das Gupta stood firm. "That is out of the

question, Dr. Gillet. We are not bloody murderers like our enemies. We do not deal in any violence we can avoid, and certainly not in cold-blooded killing merely to prevent a possible future danger. It is that kind of thinking that we fight against. No, we will hold them, talk to them, try to reason with them to see our cause."

Gillet shrugged. "As you wish, Master Govinda. But I fear you will live to regret your weakness in this matter. However, I will insist that my own guards take charge of them. They have much more experience with dangerous and totally immoral men like Carter and Shelby."

Das Gupta nodded. "That is agreed, Dr. Gillet. My young people have much still to learn."

Almost unseen by Carter, a squad of AV soldiers had come silently into the reactor room. Two of them were Europeans, with the stripes of sergeants on their unmarked camouflage fatigues and gold berets. They would be training cadre, probably professionals from some European army or mercenary unit. The other ten were Indians, but they looked older and a lot harder than the youths who had been massacred at Rishikesh by the elite Chinese paratroops. Scars on their heavy faces and bare arms showed a history of something other than nonviolence.

"Take them back to the tower room," Gillet ordered. "And guard the door and the foot of the stairs. Change men every hour."

The two Europeans came to take Carter's and Shelby's arms to search them. One of the sergeants suddenly jumped back, his AK-47 up and leveled at the Killmaster.

"Ach! This one has a knife in his sleeve!" he cried in German. The professional soldier glared at Das Gupta. "Didn't your men search him before you brought him here?"

"They were searched," Lalita admitted, "but our young men do not have your skill, Sergeant Schlacke."

The sergeants confiscated Hugo, but they made their own mistake. Soldiers, not policemen, they failed to pat Carter down inside his thigh and missed the tiny gas bomb. With a nod to the hard-looking Indians of the older AV unit, they left with Carter and Shelby secure among them.

As he left, Carter stared at Lalita Chatterjee. The woman averted her eyes, and Govinda Das Gupta was biting his lip.

In the stone room with its mats and single high window, Shelby and Carter listened to Georg Gillet's special squad's footsteps fade away down the long flight of narrow stone steps that had no doors or windows the entire way to the ground a hundred feet below.

"So," Shelby said, stretched out calmly on a mat, "what do you suggest this time?"

"We wait until about midnight," Carter said. "Then we get out of here."

Shelby nodded. "Excellent plan. You have wings?"

"You might say that. But getting out of here isn't the problem. Even getting out of the temple isn't the problem."

"So what is the problem?"

"How to stop Gillet, the AV, and that breeder reactor from turning the subcontinent into a battleground at best, and a holocaust at worst, that could drag in the whole damn world."

The big agent turned on his side on the mat, propped on his elbow, and shook his head at the Killmaster. "The job, Carter? Important, but there's nothing we can do unless we can get out of here and out of the temple. The way I see it, if you think we really can get out of here, is we head straight for my bosses in Delhi and Langley and bring back the marines. This isn't a job or the time to do it alone. If we try, and fail, they can go on with their plans with no one knowing a damn thing until it's too late."

"It's already too late, Shelby," Carter said. "Any attack from outside and Gillet would let that reactor blow before he gave up. I know his history, and he's more of a fanatic than Das Gupta or any of the Indians. He's got his own plans and his own private protection. My bet is Das Gupta and the AV mean nothing to him, just dupes for his own purposes while he's out to help them re-establish the golden age of India."

"You think it's his own golden age he has in mind?"

"In spades."

Shelby nodded. "All right, Carter, we'll play it your way if you can get us out of here. Meanwhile, we should get some sleep. It could be a long night."

At the high window, Nick Carter listened. The entire temple seemed sunk in complete silence. The angle of the moon told the Killmaster it was just about midnight.

"Ready?"

"For the last five hours," Shelby said. "Make your miracle."

Carter grinned. He came down from the high window, removed his left shoe, and took off the thick heel. Inside lay a coil of thin nylon-coated wire.

"A hundred feet, load strength three hundred pounds."

"A good thing," Shelby said, looking down at his bulky body. Then he shook his head in admiration. "You're something else, Carter. Anything we can't do or aren't prepared for?"

"Let's hope we never find out."

Then Carter took off his other shoe and extracted a small clamp with a thin superstrong steel hook attached. He clamped the hook on the end of the wire, and handed it to Shelby who hooked the thin cord to the heavy metal door handle. At the other end, Carter dropped the wire silently out of the high window.

"Go!" Shelby said.

Carter vaulted to the stone sill, passed the thin wire under his thigh and across the other shoulder, and rappelled silently down the side of the tower, swinging out from time to time to survey the empty courtyard below. As soon as he touched down in the blackness of the yard, he released the thin wire.

A short time later a puffing Philip Shelby stood beside him.

"We need weapons," the big agent said the instant he had his breath back. "There's got to be an armory, and they'd keep it far from that reactor room."

"We need a telephone more."

"Your friend Hawk?"

"He'll send help," Carter said. "No matter what, we won't be able to hold this temple for long."

They moved like ghosts through the dark night of the courtyard, no sound at all coming from beyond the high walls. Wherever the temple was, it was some distance from the city, close on the banks of the river. One of a hundred temples in this land of ancient Hindu civilization that had been here for five thousand years through endless invasions from east and west.

Most of the rooms around the courtyard seemed to be sleeping quarters for the Arms of Vengeance soldiers. The devotion room with its offerings was dim and silent with flickering candles, but it was not empty. Govinda Das Gupta sat in meditation so deep his lotus position was as rigid as a trance. The leader of the Arms of Vengeance was alone, neither sound nor movement around him. But there was a shadow.

"Carter," Shelby whispered.

The Killmaster saw the shadow looming far back in the hall, its AK-47 outlined against the flickering candles: one of the European sergeants of Georg Gillet. Another shadow seemed to be off in another corner. The renegade scientist was keeping a close watch on the Hindu leader.

"What do you think Gillet really wants?" Shelby asked as they slipped out of the central temple hall.

"Power or money, international blackmail. And he doesn't plan to share either with the Arms of Vengeance but needs Das Gupta as a front."

Four guards stood at the door that led down to the hidden reactor room. If Carter and Shelby were going to get to the reactor, they were definitely going to need more armament than tiny Pierre taped to Carter's leg. The question now was how to find those weapons before their escape was discovered. There were too many guards on the reactor door to sneak up on or jump in such a limited space without weapons.

They would have to go on searching for the temple armory.

Carter was about to move away, when he heard footsteps approaching from the other end of the corridor outside the reactor room. Shelby's voice was a hoarse whisper in his ear.

"Do you think they've heard us? Spotted the escape?"

Carter shook his head. "There would be a charge. It's something else."

And it was. Four more Arms of Vengeance men appeared marching up to the reactor door. It was the changing of the guard. Carter saw the opening at once.

"They'll go back to a guardroom, and take their weapons to the armory room! Quick!"

They slipped back down the corridor, out into the courtyard, and hurried around to the entrance on the other end of the building. Inside they crouched in the dark corridor until the relieved guards came past, straggling now and yawning with fatigue, their weapons trailing. Obviously no one had yet spotted the escape.

Carter and Shelby waited until the weary guards were past and along the corridor, and then followed.

They saw the Arms of Vengeance men finally stop, unlock a door, and go in. When they came out and relocked the door, they had no weapons. They trailed away up the corridor and went into another room, then closed the door behind them. A radio began to play softly inside the room. One of the Arms of Vengeance youths needed music to sleep.

"Let's get the guns," Shelby hissed.

They trotted lightly to the locked door. Shelby studied the lock. He shook his head.

"We'll need a tough bar to crack it, Carter."

The Killmaster smiled. "Or a decent lockpick."

He reached down and unclipped the buckle from his belt.

Reversed, it revealed a series of tiny lockpicks made to seem like no more than ribs in the metal. Carter studied the lock, chose the proper pick, and went to work while Shelby watched the silent doors all along the corridor. The music still played softly.

"Bingo," Carter said and pushed the door open.

In the dark room they closed the door and found the light.

"You see what I am talking about, Master Govinda?"

Shelby and Carter stood inside the door of the room with its stacked weapons and the AK-47s leveled straight at them in the hands of the ten AV soldiers.

Dr. Georg Gillet almost smiled where he stood in the very center of the weapons room with Govinda Das Gupta on one side and Lalita Chatterjee on the other.

"Well, Govinda? Are you convinced now of the danger these two represent? Had I not suspected something of this nature, some hidden equipment by the great Killmaster, they might have made good their escape and brought the entire might of our enemies down on us."

Govinda Das Gupta looked drained. "You could not try to understand, Mr. Carter? You could not trust us, Mr. Shelby?"

"It isn't you we don't trust, Das Gupta, it's your judgment in your choice of associates."

Das Gupta paled, and then erupted in anger, shouting, "You give me no choice! The Arms of Vengeance must save India from corruption!"

Lalita Chatterjee stared at Carter. "You should have given us a chance, Nick."

"You gave them every chance to understand," Georg Gillet said coldly. "Now we must remove the danger before they cause us real trouble. Before they ruin all your work, and hopes, Master Govinda. You hear me? We must kill them now!"

"Our work and hopes, or your work and hopes, Dr. Gillet?" Lalita said.

"It is not the same, my dear?" Gillet watched her with a thin smile, but she said nothing more. The turncoat scientist nodded. "It is decided then. And since you have honest reluctance to take human life except in noble battle, my own helpers will perform the executions."

He turned to look at Carter and Shelby. "Take them to a cellar room and put two men on the door. It will be at dawn. Make your peace, Killmaster."

EIGHTEEN

Gillet's German sergeant pushed Carter and Shelby into the windowless cellar room of the ancient temple. He laughed as they looked around at the bare, dank walls. There was no furniture at all in this room, no toilet, no mats on the cold, damp floor.

"These ancient Hindus knew many things about masonry, *ja*? I do not think a worm could get in or out of here, not even one as slippery as a Killmaster! So, you will be safe here, *nicht wahr*? We are sorry that there is no bed or table, but you will soon not need such things."

The German mercenary laughed again, and backed out with his hard-faced Arms of Vengeance guards. Carter looked at the silent Indians, and spoke in Hindi.

"Why do I get the feeling that Master Govinda is no longer master around here? There seems to be a change of leadership going on. Is that what you all want? Gillet as the guru?"

"Keep your mouth shut!" the German snarled. "Take the few hours you have left, Carter. This time there is no way out for you. It is finished. "*Kaput*."

161

Carter watched only the Indians, and saw a faint flicker of doubt on even the scarred faces of these older AV men.

"A firing squad at dawn? By the book, right, sergeant? The Nazis never did have any imagination, were hopelessly proper and middle-class. Order and routine above all. Bookkeepers. Your Dr. Gillet will probably even offer us the last breakfast, a cigarette, a blindfold."

The German shrugged now. "Sneer, Killmaster, you will be dead a long time."

The sergeant pushed the silent Indian AV men out and slammed the solid steel door with a heavy clang that sounded like the knell of doom.

Alone, the two agents looked around the tiny room once more. They saw nothing but stone and damp and the encrusted mineral deposits of centuries.

"How long do you think?" Shelby asked, his voice light and easy, even cheerful.

"Three hours exactly," Carter said. "When Gillet says dawn, he means dawn. I wasn't kidding the sergeant. That middle-class, proper, orderly mentality was what beat the Nazis almost as much as the Soviet stubbornness and winter, the American industrial power and imagination. Now he'll give us three hours to get out of here and beat him."

Shelby laughed lightly. "You think it's going to make any real difference, Carter?"

"Give a man time, and you give him a chance."

The Killmaster reached into his pants, dug beside his testicles, and brought out Pierre. "There's enough gas in here to put ten men to sleep."

"You amaze me again," Shelby said. "It'll do the trick!"

"No, it won't," Carter sighed. "It would do us in, too. It's lethal as all hell."

"Back to square one," Shelby said, and shrugged. "Still, if we can get out of here, and into that reactor room, it could do the job there." The big agent turned to the walls of the pitch-dark room. "Meanwhile, let's see what we really have here."

For an hour they went around the damp, encrusted walls inch by inch. They found nothing. There was no question in the minds of either of the agents that Gillet would have them executed, and that Govinda Das Gupta, reluctant though he might be, would go along with it. Another hour, and they still found no weak spot. There wasn't even an air vent or drain.

"We've got only one chance," Shelby said at last as he sat down against the dark wall. "We'll have to jump the guards."

"They'll be Gillet's special squad," Carter said. "I doubt that we'd have much of a chance. Unless we got to them about Gillet taking over from Das Gupta, or unless I can make them scared of the gas bomb, and not realize I can't use it with the two of us in the same room. . . ."

Shelby sat up straight. "That just might work. They won't be expecting us to have a weapon. Especially that sergeant. He's a trained soldier. If we threaten to use it, he'll assume it can't hurt us."

"I think you've got it," Carter agreed. "Okay, they'll be here in one hour. Now, what we'll—"

The Killmaster stopped. Shelby froze. Outside they heard the sound of heavy footsteps coming down stone steps and then approaching the steel door.

"They're an hour early!" Shelby groaned.

"Get ready," Carter said, holding Pierre out of sight behind his thigh.

The lock clicked, and the heavy door swung open with a loud clang. Three Arms of Vengeance men came in. The leader was not the German sergeant. Carter looked at Shelby. The other two weren't Gillet's hard-bitten Indians. The one in charge was a slightly older Indian youth, his two men a pair of the normal young Arms of Vengeance recruits.

"I am sorry," the pale leader of the squad said nervously. "Master Govinda says it is time. You are to have half an hour in the hall of Krishna to make peace with your gods.

He is sorry, but it is all he can do. Our quest for peace must come first."

Carter nodded. "We understand, son," he said in Hindi, smiled, and took Pierre from behind his leg. "But we don't feel much like making peace just now. This is a gas bomb. It will kill you all in seconds. You'll drop those rifles now!"

The three youths went white, and stared at the small bomb in Carter's hand. Then the older leader seemed to stiffen, and he shook his head slowly.

"We are not afraid to die. We must fulfill our trust, sir. For the honor of Krishna and Arjuna the warrior, we cannot allow you to escape. Your bomb may kill us, but our brothers beyond the door will stop you."

For a moment, the three youths and the two agents faced each other. Then Carter slowly lowered the gas bomb. The integrity of the youths had beaten him, where the cynical and worldly experience of the German sergeant wouldn't have.

"You will please to give me the bomb, and go out now, sir," the AV leader ordered.

"I'm sorry, son," Carter said. "I guess we'll all go together."

The Killmaster held the little egg-shaped bomb in front of him, his hand on the pin.

"No!"

The shout came from outside the room. There was a flurry among the young AV soldiers out there, and Lalita Chatterjee came pushing through. She stood in front of the young AV leader.

"We are wrong, Sardhu," she said fervently. "Dr. Gillet is using us, I know that now. The Master is wrong. He desires our cause of love and peace so much, desires to place the world on the path of truth and peace, that he has allowed his human weakness to blind him. Think, Sardhu, the rest of you. We do not execute people! We do not build bombs, and Carter has told the truth. The only use for plutonium is for a bomb! Gillet wants only power or money or both. His karma is an evil karma. His path is false."

One of the youths from outside stood behind her. "She is right, Sardhu. She speaks the truth. We have already joined with her. Come with us. You cannot take this man and send him to sure death. Join with us all and help Master Govinda to see his terrible error."

The older youth looked at Lalita, and at the young Arms of Vengeance men around her. They were all nodding now. All five of them. But he slowly shook his head.

"I understand, but I cannot join with you. It would not be honorable for me. I have been trusted with a mission by the Master, and I cannot deny his orders. Please, you will all leave and lock me into this room. I will stay here until someone comes. If you have not all escaped by then, I must fight you, but now you will go and leave me."

Lalita nodded. "We honor you, Sardhu. Nick, Mr. Shelby, come with us. Quickly now."

They locked the room door with the solitary young leader inside and hurried up the stairs and out into the dark courtyard that was pitch-black now an hour before dawn. Lalita led them across the courtyard.

"What changed your mind, Lalita?" Carter asked,

"The truth, Nick. Master Govinda's vision of the Arms of Vengeance was good, and most of those involved are men and women of true faith in peace and love. But Gillet has used us. He is a conniving, manipulating man who thinks only of himself; I know that now. He will say anything, do anything, to get what was denied him as a young man. He is consumed only with hate and greed and ambition. Here in India we have many factions, and much fanaticism, and a great tendency to violence, but I now know that it is all this that the way of Krishna is against. That when the Charioteer spoke of right action, he meant the action of truth and peace and love. Somewhere, the cult of the warrior has led Master Govinda astray."

"Does Das Gupta know you've switched, Miss Chatterjee?" Shelby panted as he limped to keep up.

"No," she said.

"He still doesn't agree with you?" Carter asked.

The beautiful Indian agent shook her head. "I have tried, Nick, but he cannot give up his dream. He knows that the only way he could oppose Gillet now would be to destroy the Arms of Vengeance itself."

"Then it's up to us," Carter said grimly. "How many men do you have?"

"Men? Only you and Mr. Shelby," she said. "The rest are boys."

"How many boys, then?"

"I have convinced eight so far. But it doesn't matter. You must escape. Gillet has his private killers, and Master Govinda will not stop Gillet. I think we are enough to overpower the guards at the gate and get you and Mr. Shelby away. I will stay, and try to fool Gillet long enough for you to bring back the authorities. But there is little time."

"Time?" Carter watched her in the dark night as they moved toward the outer gates. "Gillet doesn't know you convinced Das Gupta to let us have time to pray, does he? He'll send his men for us in half an hour."

"Or less."

"And when he finds us gone, he'll kill you, maybe Das Gupta, and set the reactor to go critical after he gets away," Carter said. In the dark night he stopped. "No, Lalita. We can't escape. We've got to shut down that reactor. No arguments. Where are the rest of your men?"

"At the armory room."

"Let's go."

They retraced their steps back into the dark and silent building and along the same corridor where the single door down into the reactor room was. Two of Lalita's converts guarded the armory. Inside, they made their plan.

"There are still four guards at the reactor door," Lalita said. She looked at her watch. "The change is due to come in half an hour. I think if I go with four of my boys, we can convince the guards we've come early because of the executions at dawn."

"Unless they are Gillet's men," Shelby cautioned.

Lalita shook her head. "Gillet always keeps his special squad with him. He will send them to get you for the execution, but right now he'll have them with him."

"Do you know where he is?" Carter asked.

"No, Nick. I wish I did. We could try to get to him outside the reactor room."

"It's safer to shut down the reactor. Then, even if he escaped us, he couldn't get it going again fast enough to do any damage. Okay, we send your four to take over the door. Do we have a key to the door?"

"Yes, I do," Lalita said.

"Then once we have the door secured, we all go down as fast as we can. At this hour there shouldn't be more than a skeleton crew on duty. Probably one of those Cuban women scientists to watch the dials and gauges, and maybe one or two of your AV people to do whatever she needs done."

Lalita agreed. "I've never seen more than that at this hour."

Carter stood up, picked up an AK-47, and slammed home the banana clip. "Okay, then—let's take that reactor room."

Lalita formed up her four guards, and with her in the lead, they marched off down the corridor to where the four weary, yawning Arms of Vengeance youths stood outside the reactor door. They were so tired they failed even to challenge the newcomers when they saw Lalita.

"The Master has shifted the schedule by half an hour because of the executions. You are to go back to your rooms, but do not sleep. Do your ritual ablutions and prepare for the deaths to come this morning."

The four men all bowed their heads, formed up, and marched away down the corridor to the armory room. As they entered, Carter and Shelby and the others who had joined Lalita disarmed them, then asked if they wanted to join too. One did, but the rest were too afraid. Carter had them tied up, then he hurried along to the door down to the reactor room where Lalita waited with her four youths.

"Ready?"

They all nodded.

"Down!"

Carter leading, they all ran down the narrow flight of stairs into the bright, clean, air-conditioned reactor room. Carter burst out of the doorway and turned toward the console.

Georg Gillet looked up.

The renegade German-American scientist and Carter stared at each other for a long moment.

Throughout the reactor room his ten men sat and lounged; the two Cuban women scientists worked over dials. There was some kind of experiment in progress, so all Gillet's people were in the reactor room. Gillet saw Lalita Chatterjee.

"So? A *double* traitor, Miss Chatterjee? That is too bad. Now you will have to die with Carter and Mr. Shelby. You and all your young men."

Carter raised his AK-47. "Any move, and it won't be one of us who dies, Gillet."

The scientist shook his head. "My hand is on a button, Carter, that will instantly begin an irreversible reaction to bring the reactor critical and out of control. One shot, and you will destroy Kamarpuri, most of Utter Pradesh, and the millions and millions who live on the Ganges. Do you understand?"

Carter said nothing. Gillet barked an order.

"Sergeants! Kill them!"

Carter and Shelby both fired. The German sergeants clawed for the floor. Everyone in the room took cover. Everyone except Gillet.

"Back!" Carter commanded. "Back up the stairs!"

Lalita, Shelby, her young Arms of Vengeance soldiers, and Carter all ran back up the stairs and out into the corridor before anyone in the reactor room could recover. They slammed the door shut.

"What now, Nick?" Lalita rasped.

"We've got him trapped down there," Shelby said. "Maybe we can get help now."

The big agent turned for the door out into the courtyard.

"There they are!" voices cried out in Hindi.

There was a wild fusillade of fire.

Out in the dark courtyard they saw all the rest of the Arms of Vengeance soldiers with Govinda Das Gupta standing among them.

NINETEEN

It was a Mexican standoff.

The Killmaster, Shelby, Lalita, and the Arms of Vengeance youths who had joined her held the corridor outside the only door down to the reactor room.

Gillet, the two Cuban scientists, and his ten hard-nosed mercenaries held the reactor room.

Das Gupta and the main body of Arms of Vengeance soldiers held the courtyard and the rest of the temple.

With both cross corridors covered, there was no way Das Gupta and his young, raw recruits were going to dislodge or overcome Carter and Shelby.

Gillet could hold the single entrance to the reactor room against ten times his number, and, with his finger on the reactor button, no one could try a direct assault anyway.

Das Gupta had too many men, even if they were raw and barely trained, for Carter's small group to overcome them or even break out.

An attack from outside would have to get through Das Gupta to reach Carter and Shelby, and any such attack could make Gillet decide to go out in a blaze of radioactive glory.

"What do we do, Nick?" Lalita wanted to know.

"Not a damn thing," Shelby said cheerfully, "except wait 'em both out, and hope someone heard the shooting and sends enough aid to help."

"Is there a telephone that's working in the temple?" Carter asked.

"Yes, Nick."

"Take me to it."

The phone was in the small business office that even a temple swami must have to conduct the mundane everyday affairs of the modern bureaucratic world. Carter dialed in his various codes, and after a long delay and much beeping and clicking on the antiquated Indian equipment, Hawk's gruff voice came on.

"Where the hell have you been, N3? We've got World War Three hanging over us with Chinese, Indian, and Soviet border clashes! Beijing and Delhi are at each other's throats. Pakistan is massing on the Indian border, and Langley's breathing fire over the Arms of Vengeance. What the devil's going on?"

Carter filled in the irascible chief of AXE as fast as he could, and explained the situation at the temple near Kamarpuri as bluntly as possible.

Hawk was silent for almost a minute, nothing coming over the phone from far-off Washington except the sounds of him chewing on a cigar. Then his voice came grim but quiet.

"I can get to Delhi, and our people in Karachi, within minutes, maybe faster. Beijing too. They may still have those paratroopers of theirs in the vicinity. But none of that's going to do damn all unless you can get Gillet's finger off that reactor, Nick. You understand?"

"Yes, sir."

Another silence. Not even the flick of Hawk's lighter. Just the slow, endless chomping. "If that reactor blows or melts, it'll not only wipe out Kamarpuri, contaminate most of Utter Pradesh with more millions of casualties than we can imagine in such a dense population, but it'll blow into

China and the Soviet Union, and pollute the Ganges through a third of India."

"And you can't risk sending troops until you know Gillet won't go out and take the reactor with him."

"He sounds crazy enough, Nick. We can't risk it. You've got to secure that reactor and shut it down safely, before the rest of the world can do anything."

"Got any ideas how I do that, sir?"

"Not a clue."

"Swell," Carter said.

There was one more long silence. "This is the big one, Nick. You'll do it. I'll have enough troops standing by to overrun the continent. They'll get to you in minutes or less when you give the signal the reactor's secure."

"Gotcha," Carter grunted, and slowly hung up.

It was up to them.

"Well?" Shelby said.

The big agent was prone to the corridor, his AK-47 trained on the reactor room door. Lalita behind him covered the rear of the corridor.

"We can have help from Delhi, Karachi, Beijing, and Moscow within minutes—*after* we shut down the reactor."

Shelby swore. Lalita laughed bitterly. The armed youths of the Arms of Vengeance who were crouched along the dim corridor only looked nervous. They did not understand the English Carter was speaking, but they sensed the grimness in their leaders.

"How do we do that, Nick?" Lalita wondered.

"Take the bit in our teeth and barge down those stairs again," Shelby said. "Some of us should get through."

Carter shook his head. "With Gillet's veterans, I doubt it. They'd key on the three of us, and if we went, these AV boys would vanish like smoke. Besides, if even one of us got to Gillet, he'd pull the plug, turn the reactor critical, and pollute half of India."

"Then . . . ?" Shelby said.

"I can think of only one way." Carter turned to Lalita.

"Can we shut down the power to the reactor? Turn everything off so it has to remain dormant?"

Lalita thought. "I'm not sure, but I think so. I mean, I know there is a main electrical box down in the cellar, but—"

"But?"

"The only way into the cellar is through the courtyard, and the box is right next to the reactor room with a door into the room from the cellar right near it."

They all let that sink in. Then Carter shrugged. "I've heard worse. We have to do it. I'll go alone. When—"

"No, you won't," Lalita said. "We'll have a much better chance if we go together. Master Govinda can't be totally sure I've changed my spots all the way yet. I know where the entrance is, and I can talk to most of the AV youngsters in case we run into trouble."

"Okay." Carter had no choice but to agree. "Let's go, then. You hold the fort, Shelby."

"It'll be here when you get back," the big agent said.

A thin dawn light bathed the courtyard. The youths of Das Gupta's small army dozed at their positions covering all the exits from the temple.

Carter and Lalita Chatterjee slipped low and close to the gray stone building. With the overhang of the roof they were in the shadows, and Das Gupta's amateur soldiers were more asleep than alert. They saw no sign of Das Gupta himself now.

Narrow steps behind an iron railing led down to the basement.

"There it is." Lalita nodded to the narrow black rectangle ahead.

There was no one posted to guard the cellar entrance.

"Das Gupta is no soldier," Carter said.

"That's what Gillet told him."

"Do they have any good military leaders?"

"At some of the other camps."

"Lucky for us."

Down the narrow stairs they found the steel door at the bottom locked. Carter used the lockpicks from his buckle, and they slipped inside.

In the pitch-dark cellar they stood and listened. Gillet's men weren't amateurs. With a door into the reactor room from the cellar, they could have a man outside it.

Carter and Lalita knew before they went in what they had to do. They separated, and Lalita made a sharp sound of metal against metal.

Carter waited, his assault rifle ready.

Lalita made another sound.

Nothing happened.

Once again.

Silence.

Lalita switched on her flashlight.

The cellar was deserted.

"Let's find it fast," Carter said.

The vast, dusty cellar was packed with the debris of centuries. They moved as silently as possible around the walls looking for where the modern intrusion of a fuse box and main switch had been installed among the ancient ghosts.

"There, Nick."

It was an old British-made fuse box with a newly installed extra-large conduit-covered line entering the reactor room. A new circuit breaker controlled the massive new power source for the reactor.

"That makes it easy," Carter announced with a smile. "We can cut down the reactor alone. Throw the breaker and stand back."

Lalita threw the breaker, and Carter used all his strength to pull the heavy cable out of the box.

"Come on!"

They ran across the dark cellar by the single beam of Lalita's flashlight. The moment the power shut off in the reactor, Gillet's men would be out to see what had happened.

They were at the door out.

Nothing had happened.

Carter stopped.

"Why haven't they reacted?" Lalita wondered.

Carter shook his head in the eerie light of the single flashlight beam. "Listen."

As they stood in the ancient cellar they could hear the steady hum and throb. The reactor was still running.

"Backup generator power," Carter muttered. "It's standard, but I'd hoped Gillet wouldn't have been able to have it here."

"How long will it last, Nick?"

"Long enough," Carter said grimly. "We'll have to think of another way."

"But," Lalita cried in dismay, "there isn't any other way!"

"There has to be. Let's get back."

They slipped out the door and up to the courtyard. The morning had turned to a full gray light now. Das Gupta's young Arms of Vengeance soldiers were stirring and yawning all around the yard. Carter and Lalita were halfway back to the entrance door into the temple they had left half open when the cry went up in excited Hindi.

"There! It is the American and the traitor!"

"Run for it!" Carter shouted.

He and Lalita sprinted for the dark opening. A wild, ragged volley sang over their heads, sending chips flying from the ancient gray stone. Before there was time for a second, more accurate, volley, they both dived in through the opening and swung the door shut behind them.

On their feet, they hurried back to where Philip Shelby waited in the corridor outside the door down into the reactor room. All along the still dark corridor the few Arms of Vengeance youths who had joined them dozed.

"Luck?"

"All bad," Carter said, and told the big agent everything that had happened in the cellar, including the backup generator power he had hoped would not be there. "We'll have to find another way to get down there without a head-on attack."

The soft voice spoke in its Hindi-accented English.

"I don't think you, Mr. Shelby, or our Lalita will be able to do that, Mr. Carter."

Govinda Das Gupta stood in front of a door that had opened in the center of the corridor. His men poured from the open door behind him and spread out in both directions, taking the few youths loyal to Lalita by surprise.

"I think it is now I who will decide what is to be done," said the small leader of the Arms of Vengeance.

TWENTY

Philip Shelby looked at the solemn Govinda Das Gupta. He looked at the massed armed youths of the Arms of Vengeance now in total control of the corridor outside the entrance to the breeder reactor room.

"Who let them in?" The big man turned on Carter, then on Lalita Chatterjee. "There was no way they could get into that room! I checked it out myself. One door and the windows are barred. Who did it?"

Govinda Das Gupta shook his head almost sadly. "That is the sick way of the modern world, Mr. Shelby. We cannot trust; we must suspect all of evil. If there is that which you do not understand, it must result from some human deceit, some trick, some betrayal. But perhaps there is another explanation, more honest and honorable. One you do not know. Perhaps can never know but must simply accept."

Carter looked at all the guns now in the corridor. The guns that had taken charge of what would happen unless he could somehow reverse it. "All true, Master Govinda, but how you got in here past all of us isn't one of those explanations we can never know, is it?"

Das Gupta stood silent for a time, his eyes downcast at the floor of the corridor that was now showing the rays of the early-morning sun of India from both ends and from the open door of the room Das Gupta and his AV youths had come from. When he looked up, there was pain in his soft eyes.

"I have spent most of this night in meditation. I have asked the merciful Vishnu for guidance, perhaps a sign. I have thought much and long." He raised his eyes and they hardened as he looked at Carter in the ancient temple corridor. "I have also spoken by telephone to Dr. Gillet. I have asked him to turn the temple back to me and the Arms of Vengeance. He has refused. He has said that he will destroy the reactor and unleash a horror on my country if we do not all leave and send the leaders of India to speak with him."

"Money," Shelby said. "He knows the Arms of Vengeance is over for him, so he'll try to blackmail the country now."

Das Gupta's small face was in pain. "It is now clear to me that Dr. Gillet is not an honest or honorable man. He never had any belief in our cause, and wished only power for himself. Miss Chatterjee has done the correct thing, and now I must also do what must be done."

"Master—" Lalita began.

The little man raised his hand. "Do not feel distressed. I have decided that my vision was incorrect. That the way of the warrior has led us into the same errors of blood and violence that belong to our opponents. I know now that we cannot reach the path of tranquillity through the pain and suffering of others, even our enemies. The Arms of Vengeance will end for now. When they rise again it will be as warriors of courage but also of love." He turned to look at all his youths in their golden berets in the morning sun. "You will all put down your weapons. We are now all one here."

Lalita smiled. Shelby looked relieved. Only Carter did not smile or relax.

"We still have a major problem, Das Gupta, before you decide to shut down the dream and walk away," Carter said. "There's a little toy you've helped to create still down there in that room."

"Yes, Mr. Carter, of that I am most painfully aware. It is a problem, we will, I hope, solve together."

"How?" Shelby demanded. "Are you going to lead the charge yourself, Master Govinda?"

Das Gupta smiled for the first time. "I am not quite the fool you think me, Mr. Shelby. No, we will make our attack the same way I and my young men came into this corridor. The way you could not explain, eh?"

"Passages," Carter guessed. "Old hidden passages from the ancient times."

"Yes," Das Gupta said, nodding. "A passage comes from the outside into that room, just as one leads from our armory room into the room below where Gillet built his reactor."

"How close to the reactor?" Carter asked quickly.

"Across the entire room," Das Gupta said. "Hidden behind much piping, but far from the controls."

"So we still have the problem of Gillet letting it run away if he feels he's finished."

"And that he would do," Das Gupta agreed.

"Then," Shelby said, "we will simply have to move very fast."

"We'll have to do more than that," Carter said. "Gillet doesn't know yet we're all together. That's what we'll use. It'll be close and risky, but we have to try. I think I've got a plan that will work. Now, what we'll do is . . ."

In the morning light of the corridor, the Indian sun all the way up now, Carter, Shelby, Lalita Chatterjee, and Govinda Das Gupta crouched on the floor and made their plan.

In the soundproof, windowless, air-conditioned breeder reactor room, Dr. Georg Gillet smiled where he sat at the control console, his hand an inch away from the button that would send the reactor critical and out of control. What an

arrogant American fool this Carter was to think he could
defeat Georg Gillet with such an infantile ruse as cutting off
the main power. He almost laughed aloud, and thought of
his father.

*"You must plan, Georg, always plan for everything. Plan
and understand what is possible and have always an
alternate plan for successful retreat to attack again. The
mistake the Führer made was to overreach in Russia and
then to have no plan for defeat. Remember, other people do
not always act as they should and therefore no plan can be
perfect. The winner is the man with an alternate plan for
temporary defeat as well as victory."*

So he had made sure of the backup power self-contained
in the breeder room complex itself, and had prepared the
alternate plan to blackmail India and the world if the Arms
of Vengeance rebellion failed at any point. The failure had
come sooner than he had expected, thanks to the weakness
of Das Gupta and the incredible American luck of this agent
Carter, but he had been ready. The feeble attempt of Carter
to defeat him with the shutoff of power only showed how
his victory was assured.

Gillet almost relaxed where he sat. It was only a matter of
time. And not very much time. All over the world, from
Washington to Beijing, they were frantically conferring,
arguing, analyzing, studying, debating, but the fools would
realize, the smarter ones like the Chinese and Germans
almost at once, that they had no choice. They would pay,
meet his escape terms, and he would vanish to the safety of
the secret retreat in Paraguay only the old associates of his
father knew existed. He would literally drop from the
earth—until the next time. And the next time he would not
make the error of choosing to work with a weakling like Das
Gupta.

"Sir?"

She stood in front of him, her eyes nervous and her face
uneasy. Gillet was irritated. The waiting was beginning to
get on his nerves, and he had never really adjusted to female
scientists.

"Yes, Señora Silva? You have some problem with the reactor?"

"No, sir," Gabriela Silva said, "not with the reactor."

"With what, then?"

"I came here to work with Master Govinda because I was not happy with the militant and violent direction being taken by Dr. Castro at home. Now I am concerned that we are departing from Master Govinda's aims. Why is he not here with us to stop this American warmonger from destroying our plans?"

"Ah, but he is, my dear." Gillet smiled while he raged inside. *The stupid bitch!* There was the trouble. Emotions, when cool logic must prevail. Das Gupta would fail, he knew that now, and so should she. "The Master is outside in the courtyard. He will attack and destroy the American, the Englishman, and the Indian traitoress at dawn. The problem will be over. But we had to protect the reactor, or the American could have blackmailed us all."

"Did I not hear you tell Master Govinda you would no longer do as he wished?"

Gillet laughed. "A ruse, my dear. To lull the American. We both knew he was listening. Master Govinda wants to take them alive and without bloodshed so the Arms of Vengeance can remain pure."

"I see, yes." Gabriela Silva nodded slowly, brightening. "That would be the way of the Master."

"Then I must ask you to return to your post. It could all be over momentarily, and then we must go back to work on making the plutonium we need to force the world to make peace."

All the time Gillet talked to the older Cuban woman, he had been aware of the younger one, Luisa Paz, watching them. The younger woman, much tougher and yet more sensual, was not as good a scientist, but Gillet had other plans for her. She would be the one person he would take with him. The two ex-German sergeants if he could, but they were expendable if that had to be. Only young Señorita

Paz would be good to have with him in Paraguay while he worked and waited for the next opportunity.

Gillet glanced at his watch. What was taking the fools so long? They had to know they were beaten. There was nothing they could do but pay him his ransom and meet all his demands for his escape.

His long fingers drummed impatiently inches from the button that could initiate a nuclear disaster far worse than any the world had seen. The deaths of millions all down the mighty Ganges. The magnitude of it took his breath away with pride.

But it would not happen. As his father had taught him—*"Power is what counts, Georg, only power. Do not be seduced by pride, or accomplishment, or glory, or achievement. Power can gain a man all these things and the one indispensable factor nothing else can—the right to do exactly what you want exactly how you want."*

His fingers drummed on.

What the devil was taking so long?

They could not be so foolish as to try to stop him? No, no one could be that stupid.

Up in the now sunny corridor outside the single entrance to the reactor room, Govinda Das Gupta looked at his watch. He nodded to the older youths who led his young Arms of Vengeance warriors. The small Hindu's face seemed to glow. He knew, now, that he was doing what had to be done. The eager young men all around him shared the glow at last. It was time to find the greatness in their karma, follow their dharma.

"It is time," Das Gupta said. "For Krishna the Charioteer. We are his warriors."

Das Gupta opened the door and started down into the reactor room.

Nick Carter, Philip Shelby, Lalita Chatterjee, and five of the older Arms of Vengeance youths had dropped through the hidden trapdoor in the armory room, and moved silently through the inky darkness of the dank, ancient tunnel. They did not want to risk even a flashlight beam that might be seen by someone. The soft singing of rats, the scurrying of small feet, seemed to be all around them. But they had work to do, and moved on until they came at last to the section of stone wall Das Gupta had diagrammed for them. On the other side was the reactor room.

Balance on a hair by the skill of the ancient Indian stonemasons, it unlatched with a simple iron bar latch.

Carter glanced around at the vague shapes in the darkness of the passage used once by Hindu priests to escape and hide from their Moghul oppressors.

"Ready?"

The seven vague heads nodded.

Carter checked the luminous dial of his watch.

"Fifteen seconds."

They tensed, each one starting the slow count inside: One . . . two . . . three . . .

Georg Gillet looked up sharply.

"Sergeants!"

The two Germans jumped to his side, AK-47s up.

The voice came from the top of the stairs.

"It is I, Dr. Gillet. Govinda Das Gupta. Carter and the others are my prisoners. The Indian government has agreed to consider your demands. They have asked me to reason with you once more. I am coming down."

Gillet froze. A trick? He glanced around quickly and saw that all his people were at their posts, armed and alert. What could a weakling like Das Gupta do? Besides, the little Hindu would make a good hostage. One more pressure on the world to do what he wanted it to do.

"Very well, Master Govinda, come down."

Das Gupta appeared at the foot of the stairs.

"So, they know they are beaten, Das Gupta. My demands remain as they were. And now I have you, too. Sergeant, take him."

Gillet laughed aloud.

"That will not be necessary, Dr. Gillet," Das Gupta said. "I come to you of my own free will to try once more to make you see that the ways of violence—"

Only as Govinda Das Gupta walked slowly toward him, talking all the way, ignoring the German sergeant with his weapon, did Georg Gillet realize he had been tricked.

He saw the Arms of Vengeance youths appear suddenly at the foot of the stairs behind the small, soft-eyed man.

"Sergeants! Everyone!"

His long fingers picked up the deadly little Uzi from the console, and he aimed it straight at Govinda Das Gupta.

TWENTY-ONE

". . . fifteen . . . *Go!*"

The massive wall swung like a feather at a single touch.

Carter hurled through, out of sight behind the massed banks of heavily insulated pipes. He raced left on the shortest route to the control console across the vast room.

Lalita Chatterjee plunged to the right around the bank of pipes followed by all five Arms of Vengeance youths with their weapons.

Shelby clumped behind Carter in as fast a run and hop as he could in his cast.

As the attackers from the secret entrance came around the pipes into the reactor complex, everything seemed to freeze. For an endless instant the whole vast room of tanks, jacketed reactor vessel, dials, gauges, recorders, pipes and flashing, beeping lights hung suspended in time and space and motion.

Govinda Das Gupta stood halfway between the door of the stairs down and Georg Gillet at the console. The small Hindu seemed to almost fill the room with his gentle face and commanding integrity, the naked courage and soft love of his eyes.

Georg Gillet held his Uzi, his finger already tightening on the trigger of the deadly little submachine gun.

The Arms of Vengeance youths with their AK-47s were packed in the doorway behind Das Gupta, a few already turning to fan out into the large room.

Gillet's two German sergeants were side by side in the center of the room. They had their weapons aimed at the AV youths in the doorway from the stairs behind Das Gupta, but their ears heard Lalita Chatterjee and her five AV men behind them.

The two female Cuban scientists were on opposite sides of the big room. The younger, Luisa Paz, far across the room from Gillet, had already abandoned her task of analyzing the data on a circular graph chart to take a pistol from her white laboratory smock.

Gabriela Silva, only a few feet from Gillet, stood as wide-eyed as a statue in her white smock.

The eight renegades from the Arms of Vengeance who had joined Gillet were scattered around the room. Some sat. Some stood. Some lounged against the walls. One had been flirting with the younger Cuban scientist.

In that motionless, silent instant, only the Killmaster moved. He ran in long strides toward where Georg Gillet sat at the console next to the button that could send the reactor into uncontrolled critical mass and destroy them all in a searing flash of heat that would send radioactive death into four countries and down the Ganges with its millions.

Then the room seemed to erupt in a thousand chaotic motions and acts of violence.

One sergeant sprayed a volley at the massed AV youths who poured from the narrow stairway into the reactor room.

The youths fell in their own blood, but those behind them continued to pour into the room diving right and left and opening fire on their renegade comrades who clawed for their weapons in panic. The young warriors for Krishna the Charioteer pressed on with amazing bravery.

The second sergeant whirled to face Lalita and her men.

The Indian agent cut him down with a fusillade from her British assault weapon.

All through the room the renegade AV and the loyal AV were fighting it out.

Luisa Paz blasted at the running Carter with her pistol.

Shelby, behind Carter, exploded her head with a single burst.

Through it all the Killmaster never looked right or left as he raced straight for Georg Gillet and the button that could destroy a billion people, some instantly, and many more slowly.

Gillet, in a split second of reflex anger, rage, and arrogance, made his final mistake. His cruel lip curled in violent hate as he shot Govinda Das Gupta down in a shattering hail of blood and bone. The force of the hail of bullets flung the little Hindu, who had dreamed of a return to the glories of his heritage, across the bloody room to sprawl in a heap at the feet of his horrified Arms of Vengeance youths.

Only then did Gillet realize his mistake.

He dropped the Uzi, clawed for the button.

Carter slammed into him like a human battering ram and the two men sprawled across the room in a tangle of arms and legs. Each came up scrambling for his weapon.

The lethal button stood unprotected, no one close to it.

Except the still-firing German sergeant.

"Der Führer!"

The sergeant lunged for the button that would vaporize them all in an instant.

A single bullet hit him between the eyes and flung him backward, dead before he hit the floor.

Gabriela Silva stood four feet away, the Beretta automatic steady in her hand.

"Insane," she whispered. "They are all insane."

"Filthy bitch!"

Dr. Georg Gillet, his face contorted with rage, grabbed

his Uzi again and cut the Cuban woman apart with a seemingly endless burst.

Carter and Shelby fired at the same instant, blowing the renegade physicist into a hideous pile of mangled flesh that lay curled grotesquely on the blood-slick floor.

Then there was silence.

Slowly Carter got up.

Shelby limped to the dead Govinda Das Gupta.

Lalita Chatterjee bent over the dead and dying youths of the Arms of Vengeance. Then she stood and looked around the room with its blood and carnage. The bodies of Govinda Das Gupta, Gillet, the two sergeants, the Cuban women, all eight of the AV who had joined Gillet in his final madness, and too many loyal AV youths.

She dropped her weapon.

"Maybe we *are* all crazy."

"Maybe," Carter said as he walked to her across the shattered room, "but as long as some are crazier than the rest of us, someone's got to stop them. Das Gupta had a gentle vision that got off the track, Lalita, and that laid him open for Gillet to use him." The Killmaster looked toward where the surviving Arms of Vengeance youths were wrapping their dead leader in a long cloth ready to carry him to his funeral pyre. They were all crying, their blood and wounds forgotten. "Lucky for all of us he saw what he had done in time, and had the guts and vision and truth to correct it."

"We were wrong from the start, weren't we, Nick?" Lalita said. "You can't bring peace with warriors of any kind. We didn't want peace, we wanted triumph. We were caught up in the pride of the past. I'll resign, of course."

"Don't be hasty, my dear," Shelby said, limping to her. "We all make mistakes. Sometimes we even learn from them, become stronger."

"Perhaps," Lalita said. "What will you do now, Nick?"

"Report in," Carter said. "Mission accomplished."

David Hawk and Nick Carter stood beside the helicopter

that had brought the AXE chief to Kamarpuri and the temple six miles from the city on the banks of the great Ghaghra River. Regular Indian troops swarmed over the temple, and had taken charge of all the dead and living.

"They're rounding up the Arms of Vengeance people all over the country and abroad with the help of your Miss Chatterjee and Rip Ramprasad. It seemed that that rich lover of the Hindu past has had a change of heart after a talk with the government."

"He was only playing at it," Carter said. "Radical chic and all that."

"Yes," Hawk agreed, chewing on his cigar. "They'll cover it all up, of course. It never happened. Langley is only too willing to cooperate, and save themselves a lot of embarrassment. It seems a certain Pakistani underground hero was picked up on an Indian road with a lady friend and tossed into a local slammer. Our Company friends had to pull a lot of strings to get them out and safely home to Karachi."

Carter grinned. "I hope they were kind to the lady."

"I hear she can take care of herself," Hawk said dryly. "And your Miss Chatterjee's resignation has been turned down. Looks to me like she and Shelby have a lot in common."

"I think they do, sir," Carter said. "I hope they can find even more."

"Matchmaking, Nick? You miss that kind of commitment, perhaps?"

"Sometimes, sir," Carter admitted.

Hawk chewed the cigar, then took out his lighter and lit it. "I understand. But for us, for you and me, the work must always come first."

"Always," Carter said.

"So, are you ready for your next job? I've got something that needs you in Singapore by tonight. Up for it?"

"Well, sir, I think I'd like to take a little side trip. Some leave time and all that."

"Leave?" Hawk puffed furiously.

"I've got a week coming, right? Madrid is lovely this time of year, and I have a file I've got to return to someone."

"Madrid?" Hawk said suspiciously.

The AXE director glared at his premier agent. Then he shrugged, and turned to the helicopter.

"One week, Nick, and you can find your own transportation."

Hawk climbed into the chopper and slammed the door. Moments later it faded away against the Indian sky. Carter laughed aloud. Madrid, and Manuela Torres, would be even better now.

DON'T MISS THE NEXT NEW
NICK CARTER SPY THRILLER

HELL-BOUND EXPRESS

Carter noted the number on the paper and dialed. The voice that answered was barely a whisper.

"Herr Boris Weiner, bitte."

"Ja, das ist Weiner."

"Herr Weiner, my name is Carter. I represent a distribution company in New York. We have been alerted to the quality of your work, particularly your film work, here in Austria."

"Ja?" Noncommittal.

"We have over five hundred outlets in the States, and we need product very badly . . . special product, if you know what I mean."

"I see. We would have to discuss this in person."

"Of course," Carter said. "I have an afternoon flight out. I wonder if I could meet with you right away?"

"I am afraid that would be impossible. I have—"

"Herr Weiner, I am talking in the neighborhood of all your old titles, perhaps a half million or more units a month."

"I do most of my business on this level from my house."

"I understand," Carter said. "Shall we say an hour?"

"That would be fine. The address is—"

"I have it. An hour, Herr Weiner."

Carter hung up. Elaine was staring at him open-mouthed. "What do you know about pornography?"

"That it's boring," he said with a shrug. "But product is product, no matter what it is."

Elaine had the plastic bag open on her desk. Carter dug into it and retrieved the Vela Chebsecki savings passbook, the George Nathan Coxe passport, and the safe-deposit box key.

"You can put it back. I'll call in every hour or so."

"Nick . . ."

"Yeah?"

"Was last night a one-nighter?"

He smiled. "I hope not."

The discreet brass plate beside the thick oaken door read BORIS WEINER. The building was four stories, postwar, and in a top-drawer neighborhood across from Esterhazy Park.

The door lock buzzed, he entered, and as there was nowhere else to go, he climbed the narrow, red-carpeted stairs. At the top, a young black man, in a powder-blue uniform a size too small for his broad shoulders and bulging biceps, blocked the way.

"Your name, Mein Herr."

"Carter. I think I have an appointment." He got a welcoming smile full of perfect, pearl-white teeth and a motion to follow.

The man led him along a corridor toward the rear of the building, and opened a door padded with real leather. Carter walked into a large, high-ceilinged room full of soft light, soft furniture, and a subtle blend of perfume, incense, and Turkish tobacco.

For a moment he thought he was alone, but a short, chubby man materialized from an oversize armchair and minced his way across the room.

"Herr Carter, a pleasure to meet you, a great pleasure."

"Herr Weiner." Carter shook the limp, slightly damp hand, and resisted the impulse to wipe his palm on his trousers.

"Sit, sit, please. A drink?"

"Beer, perhaps."

Weiner snapped his fingers. "Nadu, a beer for our guest. My usual."

The black glided toward a bar in the far wall, and Weiner settled into a sofa across from Carter.

Carter wasn't sure what he had expected the king of Austrian pornography to be, but it wasn't this.

Weiner was wearing a fitted, knee-length housecoat that looked as if it had been made out of a Chinese mandarin's coat, and if the heavy gold embroidery was the real thing, he would need a bank vault instead of a closet to keep it in. Under it, he had on black silk slacks and his small feet were encased in black leather pumps. His round face was as smooth as a baby's, and had the same pinkish glow. And it was only the receding hairline that gave away his age.

The drinks were set before them and the black took up a parade rest position by the door.

"Your health, mein Herr."

"*Na zdorov'e,*" Carter responded, and slurped the beer like a longshoreman.

Weiner's big, doelike brown eyes blinked at the Russian but he managed a smile as he sipped something red and syrupy from a long-stemmed glass. When he set it down, he rubbed his pudgy little hands together. "Now, just what is it you're particularly interested in?"

"The young women you buy out of Iron Curtain countries

and sell—probably at a huge profit—to North African brothels."

The cupid's-bow lips slitted into a razor-sharp line and the big eyes got very narrow. "Who are you?"

"I told you, Nick Carter."

"I'm afraid, Herr Carter, I'll have to ask you to leave."

"I'm afraid not. Who is your contact, Weiner? Who do you pay?"

The little man snapped his fingers. "Nadu."

The young black moved forward, sure of himself.

Carter stood slowly, his hands up, palms out. "I don't want any trouble."

Nadu relaxed. The heel of Carter's hand caught him flush on the nose. Flesh and bone spread across his features like soft jelly and blood covered the bottom half of his face. He staggered back but didn't go down.

"Kill him, Nadu."

"You shouldn't have said that, little man."

The black hadn't cried out in pain; he hadn't even whimpered. He just smiled through the blood, and a switchblade popped open in his hand with a metallic click.

Nadu feinted quickly, a step forward and a slashing pass with the knife, then a step back. Carter remained motionless, and he chuckled dryly. The laugh stirred the black's anger, and anger made him incautious. He lunged forward, and Carter leaned backward. The man followed, but he didn't keep his feet under himself. He stretched too far with the glinting knife, and allowed himself to become unbalanced. It made him slower, and diminished the span over which he could move the knife.

And the fight was over.

Carter gripped Nadu's right wrist with a quick movement, and kicked. His toe dug into the black's crotch, lifting his feet three inches off the floor. His mouth opened wide and his features twisted in agony. The scream had barely started bubbling from his throat when Carter's left struck, the knuckles twisting and bursting the lips open against the teeth.

Nadu's head snapped back, the scream choking off, and he staggered backward, falling heavily to the floor, clutching his crotch. Carter took two quick steps forward and lifted his right foot. He put his weight on his right heel and twisted it as he brought it down and dug it into the man's guts.

Nadu snapped up to a sitting position, vomit spewing from his mouth. Carter took a step back and kicked him in the face. Vomit and blood spattered as Carter's toe connected, and Nadu slammed back down to a prone position, his head cracking loudly against the floor. Carter took a step forward and stamped his foot down into the man's face. Cartilage and bone crunched under his shoe as he put his weight on it and twisted it. Nadu rolled onto his side, doubled up and jerking convulsively as he vomited, choked, and moaned weakly.

Sweat was rolling down Carter's face and breaking out on his body from the brief, furious exertion, and he was breathing heavily. He wiped his shoe on the man's shirt and looked at Weiner. The man's bottom jaw was headed for his navel, and he looked as if he were about to faint.

Carter's hands itched to squeeze that fat neck, to squeeze the truth out of him like toothpaste out of a tube. "Who's your contact, Weiner?"

"I quit, I swear it! I don't do it anymore!" the little man squeaked.

Carter moved forward quickly and sank his fist into Weiner's fat stomach. He doubled over, gagging, and Carter seized his head and brought it down hard while he brought up his knee. Weiner slumped to the floor, moaning.

"That's not what I asked."

"All right, all right. *Mein Gott,* don't hit me again! I was getting my girls out of Hamburg and Amsterdam. About two years ago I got a telephone call from a man . . ."

"His name."

"I don't know, I swear it! He said the government in Prague and Budapest wanted to get rid of some undesir-

ables, prostitutes. He could set it up. All I had to do was
handle the brokering with my North African clients."

Carter felt sick to his stomach. "What did you pay?"

"Five thousand American for each one. That included
new papers."

"Why did you quit?" Weiner's face flushed and he bit his
lower lip. Carter yanked him forward by his lapels. *"Why?"*

"One of the girls, in Tripoli. She was taping pillow talk.
Her customers were army officers. She was some kind of
spy. Two Libyans came and warned me to get out of the
business. To make their point, they bombed one of my
shops. The next time a call came, I turned the man down."

"The man on the phone, did he speak German?"

"Yes, but with a heavy accent."

"What kind of accent?"

"American."

"Did you ever meet him in person?"

"Never," Weiner blubbered. "Everything was done by
telephone. The payment was cash, a drop, usually a box at
the opera."

Carter turned his face so Weiner couldn't see the look of
disgust that had crept into it. "Do you know a woman
named Olga Sonderchek?"

"Only by name. She runs a nightclub here in Vienna.
That's where Nadu picked up the girls after they came
over."

Carter moved to the door. He spoke without looking at
the other man. "You're still alive, Weiner. If I ever hear that
you're back in the slavery business, I'll be back."

—From HELL-BOUND EXPRESS
A New Nick Carter Spy Thriller
From Jove in December 1989